CATHLEE

flirt CLUB

SQUARE
FISH

Roaring Brook Press
New York

To The Dramettes and The Venons, *Clink!*

丁4

SQUARE
FISH

An Imprint of Macmillan

FLIRT CLUB. Copyright © 2011 by Cathleen Daly.
All rights reserved. Printed in the United States of America by
R. R. Donnelley & Sons Company, Harrisonburg, Virginia. For information, address
Square Fish, 175 Fifth Avenue, New York, NY 10010.

Square Fish and the Square Fish logo are trademarks of Macmillan and
are used by Roaring Brook Press under license from Macmillan.

Library of Congress Cataloging-in-Publication Data

Daly, Cathleen.
    Flirt Club / Cathleen Daly.
        p. cm.
    "A Neal Porter Book."
    Summary: Through notes and journal entries, best friends and self-proclaimed "drama
geeks" Cisco (Izzy) and the Bean (Annie) write of the trials of middle school, as well as
their efforts to attract boys by forming a Flirt Club.
    ISBN 978-0-312-65026-1
    [1. Best friends—Fiction.   2. Friendship—Fiction.   3. Middle schools—Fiction.
4. Schools—Fiction.   5. Clubs—Fiction.]   I. Title.

PZ7.D16946Fli 2011
[Fic]—dc22

                                                                    2010027473

Originally published in the United States by Roaring Brook Press
First Square Fish Edition: January 2012
Square Fish logo designed by Filomena Tuosto
macteenbooks.com

10 9 8 7 6 5 4 3 2 1

AR: 5.5 / LEXILE: 860L

The Temple from JESUS CHRIST SUPERSTAR
Words by Tim Rice   Music by Andrew Lloyd Webber
Copyright © 1969, 1970 UNIVERSAL MUSIC CORP.
Copyright Renewed   All Rights Reserved   Used by Permission
Reprinted by permission of Hal Leonard Corporation

I Don't Know How To Love Him from JESUS CHRIST SUPERSTAR
Words by Tim Rice   Music by Andrew Lloyd Webber
Copyright © 1971 UNIVERSAL MUSIC CORP.
Copyright Renewed   All Rights Reserved   Used by Permission
Reprinted by permission of Hal Leonard Corporation

1

Wherein Cisco and the Bean Decide They Are Actually International Secret Agents and Start FLIRT CLUB

Dear Cisco,

Well, it turns out 8th-grade math is just as breathtaking and exciting as 7th-grade math. (NOT!) My math teacher, Mrs. Heinick, is a rover, so I have to write you in spurts and spasms . . . She likes to stroll down the aisles real slow—she's like a silent hovercraft or some scary sci-fi phenomenon . . . like a big floating eyeball with teeth. She thinks I'm doing Algebra—HA-HA-HA-HA. I keep furrowing my eyebrows to look like I'm deep in thought. A mathematical genius at work. Yeah, right. Numbers are not my friends. Words ARE my friends. You are my friend. Food from the school snack bar is not my friend. Hello Kitty backpacks are not my friend. Jeannie Mateo in front of me has one on right now. It's one of those plastic, tiny useless ones, and she doesn't take it off during class so I have to stare at plastic kitty face. I have the urge to lean forward and pat Jeannie's shiny, cute little backpack and go "Hello Kitty, Hello Kitty" over and over . . . She'd probably slap my hand away like it was the plague. Oh my gosh, remember that song we wrote called "I Have the Plague" last year? How'd it go?

8th grade is kinda weird, huh? For one thing, the fact that we don't have ANY classes together is tragic . . . my heart will break and fall out of the bottom of my shoes in little shattered pieces of brown glass. Why brown glass you ask? I do not know. I'm gonna slip this note in your locker; write me back AS SOON AS YOU RECEIVE IT OR I WILL EXPLODE. Actually, I probably won't explode, I'll probably implode. A whole different matter entirely.

Hi, I'm back, I actually had to do some math 'cause the hovering eyeball, aka Mrs. Heinick, just floated by.

Flower Day is next Wednesday.

Who created such an implement of torture is what I want to know. They had it when my sister went here. Probably the grown-up who came up with the idea was cute and popular when they were young and never thought about the kids who DON'T get any flowers sent to them. They didn't think about the kids who have to walk through the halls empty-handed. Grasping books instead of armfuls of flowers. Ugh. Are you sending anyone a flower? I may send Enrique Alvarez one; he's as cute as a bug and he's my lab partner in science ~ we share a microscope. I'm always compelled to look at his ear when he's looking into the microscope . . . occasionally I get bold and look at his mouth or cheek, but mostly I stick to the ear. And it's a charmer, that ear of his. If I send him a flower, I may have to sign a fake name on the card, because I could NEVER face him again if he knows I sent it. Maybe I could just sign my initials . . . or a completely made-up name, a man's name even, like "Bob Williams" or something. I could say, "Enrique, keep up the excellent schoolwork, stay cute. Love, Bob Williams." Or MAYBE I could sign it "Bean" since no one knows I'm the Bean but you. They think my name is Annie Myers and yours is Izzy Mercer-Crow, the fools!

WRITE ME BACK!!

Love,
The Bean

P.S. Nice overalls.

P.P.S. Did you get the picture I left in your locker? Thank Gump we are sharing lockers again—mine is ridiculously far from all of my classes.

Dear Bean,

I'm sitting in Center Quad. It's my free period (I wish we had ours together!!), so I can totally devote myself to writing you. Chris Jordasch turned around in French and asked if we were twins or sisters 'cause we were wearing matching overalls and T-shirts. I said, "No, we just like to match." He just stared at me, raised his eyebrows, and turned back around. With a silence that spoke a thousand deadly words! The cheerleaders wear matching outfits and no one blinks twice. Of course they shake their booties a lot and present their bosoms in those tight sweaters like their bosoms are a prize pot roast on a platter. Our matching outfits are kind of baggy. Perhaps our next matching outfits should be bosom-presenting outfits. But I'm much too modest for that. "These boobs were made for hiding, and that's just what they'll do, one of these days these boobs are gonna walk down to the zoo" (sung to "These Boots" by Nancy Sinatra). WHAT?

GOD SAVE US FROM FLOWER DAY!!!!!!!

I think you *should* send Enrique Alvarez one . . . just sign your initials, then he might just *wonder* if it was from you but never really know. You know what we *could* do? And this would have to be our deepest, darkest secret that we take to our DEATHBEDS!!!!!! *But*, we could both send each other a bunch of flowers and not sign the cards. I could probably afford to buy you 5 (they're $1.00 each, for a carnation). I send you 5 and you send me 5 and no one will ever know. They deliver them in 4th period, right? Just my luck, Madison Geller and Alanna Markley are in my 4th-period class, and they'll probably get at least 25 flowers each. I heard last year Margaret Ryan got so many she couldn't carry them all. Oh my God, my stomach hurts just thinking about it. This barbarism has to stop!! (Is "barbarism" a word? You know, like "barbaric"?) Maybe we could have a protest and carry little signs that say "STOP THE MADNESS,

DOWN WITH FLOWER DAY!!" Nahhhh . . . we'd be exiled into eternal dorkdom, and I'm just not prepared for that fate. I wish I had the courage to do something like that, but *instead* let's just buy each other flowers in a desperate attempt not to be thoroughly humiliated, OK?? I mean, I guess Flower Day is a tiny, tiny bit exciting because there is the *tiniest* possibility that we will actually get some from someone we like, or a secret admirer or something. The teeniest, teeniest, *tiniest* (is that a word?) possibility. You SHOULD get a bunch 'cause you're so smart and funny and adorable and the best girl in the world.

LOVE,
Cisco

(I think we should ENTIRELY desist in putting our real names on these notes from now on, the subject matter is too top secret, yes?)

P.S. I will deposit this note in your locker immediately, PLEASE DO NOT EXPLODE OR IMPLODE or expire in ANY WAY or I will shrivel up like those apple-head dolls we had to make in 3rd grade in Ms. Werner's class. Please write me back promptly upon receival (now I KNOW that's not a word ~ I just made it up), but don't do it during Spanish or Señor Snyder will catch you and whip you with a tortilla.

P.P.S. Muchas amor, mi amiga la cantina y sopa de banyo!

(I just made that up, what did I say?) Please translate señorita, gracias.

P.P.P.S. Please DESTROY this note when you are done.

P.P.P.P.S. I LOVE your Cisco and the Bean collage. I will make one for you.

P.P.P.P.P.S. Nice overalls.

Dear Cisco,

I'm sitting here bored out of my skull in Spanish class. I wish he WOULD whip me with a tortilla. I wish SOME-THING interesting would happen in this class. But alas, Mr. Snyder is much too mild mannered. Too bad Antonio Banderas is not my Spanish teacher, sí? He's a tub of spicy salsa if I ever saw one. *OK THEN*, it's settled . . . I buy you 5 flowers and you buy me 5—I think we can fit that into our fiscal budget. My bowels are relaxing as we speak (well, as I write). Is there any way this fine plan we are crafting can backfire? I mean, what if people find out about our covert Flower Day operation? If they catch on to our high-security, undercover, super-secret-agent-girl plan to send each other flowers, our lives are over at Wilbur Middle School, over IN A FLASH. Maybe we should sign some of the cards . . . just initials or a general friendly statement . . . maybe like "glad you're in my science class" or something? Or, I don't know, maybe "You're nice, you're sweet, here's to hoping that soon we'll meet." Forgive me. That's SOOO corny. I am such a dork . . . oh well. So what? So what, chicken butt?

Can you believe Cathy Greenwood at lunch? I LOVE our matching Shiva the Hindu God lunch boxes. Why does she talk to us now with that petulant, disturbed tone in her voice like she's just discovered caca on her blindingly white cheerleading sneakers? And what about when she goes, "Who's that on the front of them?" and we go "Shiva" . . . and she furrowed her pretty little brow and goes, "You guys are like super Jewish, aren't you?"

WHAT?

OH, BROTHER.

And then she swishes her barely-covered-with-a-cheerleading-skirt bottom away from us. Was she confusing her world religions? Was she being anti-Semitic? Was her brain removed by aliens and replaced by luncheon meat? I KNOW Cathy Greenwood is smart, she's been in honors classes with both of us for 2 years. So, what's her story? God save us from Robot Cheerleaders. God save us from Flower Day. I bet Cathy Greenwood will get about 55 flowers, eh??

OK Secret Agent no. 88, I've got to sign off before Señor Snyder discovers I am not really an 8th-grade student but a spy for an underground organization of international oddballs. Destroy this message as soon as you read it, preferably by eating it.

Love,
Annie-Bean

Dearest Secret Agent Bean,

Don't sign your real name! Remember when Grant Carson found that note I wrote you in 6th grade about my training bra and how I wondered what my breasts were being trained for? And he read it to his whole lunch table? I did not eat your last note, but I did destroy it with my special laser made especially for incinerating top-secret documents. Yes, let's sign *something* on our flower cards; no one will actually read them except us. That way, when they deliver the flowers, our little charade will look more real 'cause we can sit and read our cards . . . perhaps with a pleased little smile dancing upon our lips? (Have I been reading too much Jane Austen?) Or maybe a little *knowing* smile dancing upon our lips. Which do you think, a *pleased* smile or a *knowing* smile? Or how about a pleased AND knowing smile? Then again, what about a fiendishly delighted grin with a little drool dangling ever so delicately out of one corner of my mouth?? Nah, I'm joshing.

You know, it's hard to tell if Cathy Greenwood was actually being mean or simply clueless; she always has that pouty, petulant thing going on with her lips. She adopted that expression about the same time that her boobs grew in 6th grade . . . why does that kind of haughtiness make certain girls more popular?

And who am I to talk about HER petulant pout?

I'm sitting here trying to decide whether I should fake a *pleased* smile or a *knowing* smile when I receive a flower and a card from a FAKE admirer! OH BROTHER! Why do teen-age girls feel compelled to do strange things to their faces, twist them up into phony shapes? Does it continue into adulthood? Maybe it starts to feel natural and we can't tell anymore which of our facial expressions are real and which are fake—we lose track of our face. I hope not. Let's help each other keep track of our faces, OK? Let's shake on it.

Oh brother. You know, I realize as I've been sitting here writing this note during English (we're supposed to be writing an essay, I can do it tonight), I've been unconsciously trying out all these expressions on my face . . . the *pleased* little smile, the *knowing* little smile, the pouty, haughty expression so popular with some of the popular girls. If Mrs. Lucini saw any of it, she probably thinks I'm a wee bit bongo. "Bongo" is my new word for "crazy." I've made up two words today: "receival" and "bongo." Maybe when I'm a grown-up I can get a job as an official creator of words. Does that exist?

Anyway, I don't think Cathy Greenwood was trying to be mean, just sort of curious and ignorant . . . maybe that's wish-ful thinking. Remember in 4th grade when we were all friends and we went camping for YMCA summer camp and Cathy sat on a s'more and had melted marshmallow with a graham cracker on top stuck to her butt for, like, 15 minutes and didn't know it and when we saw it we all laughed so hard I cried and Louisa Burns peed (just a tiny bit) in her pants? Cathy laughed too, harder than anybody. That was fun.

Anyway, things change. Cookies crumble. Boobs grow. Sweaters stretch. Teachers hover. Gotta go. OK, I'll meet you by yer locker after 7th period.

Love,
Cisco aka Secret Agent No. 88

@ @ @

Dear Cisco,

That was fun yesterday—sorry Emmett is such a pain, he's having a no-TV and no-Internet week as a punishment, so he's bored and has taken to following me around like some sort of talking dog, like he used to do when he was little. I think he was spying on us 'cause he thinks you're cute.

OK, I'm gonna do it, I'm gonna send Enrique Alvarez a flower. Yikes. Here's the thing—they deliver flowers 4th period on Wednesday, and Enrique and I have Science together dur-ing 4th period and I sit directly next to him, so I can't actually sign my name 'cause I would be so embarrassed that my head would shrivel up, fall off my neck, and land in our petri dish to be examined under our microscope. Enrique is so polite and nice, he'd probably just go, "Umm, excuse me, your head fell off, and it's . . . uh . . . blocking the lens. Can I help you put it back on?" Emmett (little bro from hell) must have heard us discussing the Enrique Alvarez flower dilemma when he was spying on us 'cause at breakfast this morning, he goes to me (in a deep and manly voice with one eyebrow raised), "My name is Ricky Alvarezzzzzzz, come into my midnight abode and we will make beautiful music togetherrrrr" . . . God save us from Emmett. At least he got Enrique's name slightly wrong . . . and THANK GOD he doesn't go to our school, and what the heck is a "midnight abode"??

Oh my Gump, math is so boring. Mrs. Heinick isn't roving around the aisles today peeking over shoulders 'cause she's grading a charming little pop quiz she popped on us at the beginning of class. Today Jeannie Mateo has forsaken her Hello Kitty backpack for a soft leopard-skin one, thank God. Though I think she has her cell phone in the back pocket on vibrate 'cause her fuzzy backpack's making an occasional weird low rumbling sound. Not that I'm a big stickler for rules, but I wish she'd turned her phone completely OFF; it was BUGGING me during the quiz. What if I leaned forward and said, "Um, Jeannie, I really think that cat on your back has a fur ball," or what if I started casually petting the faux leopard fur? She'd probably screech or have a seizure—but I bet it'd probably be a cute little seizure in which her hair never got mussed and her lip gloss stayed perfectly intact. She is so well groomed and put together it's astounding. Does she visit the ladies' room between every class? Or maybe it's genetic, 'cause no matter what I do to groom, I start to fray at the edges shortly thereafter. I'm pretty much like Pigpen in the *Peanuts* cartoons. But instead of living in a cloud of dirt, I'm eternally surrounded by cat hair, random fuzz, gum wrappers, and little Post-it notes. Not to mention that EACH INDIVIDUAL curly red strand of my hair is on a personal mission (not unlike the USS *Enterprise*) to discover strange new lands and to go where no man has gone before, which is straight out from my head in a million different directions!

God save me from my own head!

Actually, sitting behind Jeannie Mateo is educational BE-CAUSE besides being so cutely coiffed, she is a MASTER OF FLIRTING. She flirts nonstop with Scott Broderson, who sits next to us. I am trying to pick up some pointers, some moves, by watching her, because the honest truth is I am a miserable failure as a flirt. I can't even *begin* to flirt. In fact, if I think someone's cute, I can hardly talk to him or look at him much less flirt with him. I mean, all I can do with Enrique Alvarez is stare at his ear. Oh, I'm a charmer all right. Oops, there's the bell—gotta go.

OK, I'm back—it's my free period now, so I can finish this in peace.

SO, I think our next undercover, secret-agent-girl operation should be learning how to FLIRT! What do you think, No. 88? We could practice on each other or Emmett (though he might barf) or even my cat. I mean, as secret agents we should be able to adopt and discard identities in the blink of an eye, yes? So, let's see if we can adopt identities that don't clam up, blush, stutter, sputter, and basically run away and die around boys. Or at least that's what I do. Perhaps I'm the one who really needs help. Anyway, let me know what you think. Your opinion is eternally valuable to me, my dearest Cisco, Secret Agent #88.

Write me back if you can, my little pork chop.

Love,
The Bean, Agent #66

Dear Beanalicious,

OK. I'm on board with the undercover learning-to-flirt operation, though I don't have a CLUE how to BEGIN to flirt, so watch Jeannie Mateo like a hawk to see what she does. She is always going steady with some boy or another, so her techniques must work . . . and of course that being perfectly coiffed and cute thing helps. We're both cute aren't we? We just need to learn how to relate to the opposite sex. Was there a course we missed somewhere along the way? Why don't they teach us things we can USE in school. Like, REALLY use?

OK, good for you for deciding to send Enrique a flower—we can work on the note together if you want this weekend. Monday's the last day to buy flowers and turn in the cards! HOLY guacamole! This Flower Day thing is slightly torturous (and a wee bit exiting). I just wish I had a crush on someone so I could send them one . . . hmm, who could I send one to? Of course, I still think Michael Maddix is a STONE FOX, but he's only going out with the most popular girl in the whole school! Oh well! No use crying over spilled milk!

No use sobbing over a sunken soufflé!

No use frowning over a melted and dripping Popsicle!

No use moping over rancid butter!

No use pouting over a dropped cheeseburger that now has little pieces of dirt and cat hair attached to the cheese!

Maybe I'll send a flower to one of those really cute popular boys. I could send one to Mick Jones just 'cause he's SO adorable and swaggery (I know, not a real word). I mean, I've never even spoken to him, I'm sure he has NO IDEA who I am, not that I'd sign my name on the card or anything . . . maybe I'd just write him a little poem. What do you think?

Anyway, I gotta keep this short, 'cause I have to use this free period to finish some homework.

See you at lunch my wild-haired (you have GREAT hair) partner in crime. Maybe we could have our first flirting practice session this Saturday?

Love,
Cisco
AKA, Your loving little pork chop

P.S. How much pork could a pork chop chop if a pork chop could chop pork?

Think upon that my friend, think upon that.

Dear Cisco,

OK, cool, come over this weekend and we'll write our notes for flower day and do our first flirting practice session. I'm excited. I'm tired of being a wallflower. I've been jotting down in my notebook observations of Jeannie Mateo flirting with Scott Broderson. Some of them may be too silly or ditsy for us; we could just try some, we'll see. Observe any flirting you see and jot it down.

Maybe we should start with my cat. That's about all I can handle. Nelson won't mind—he's such a puddle of a cat nothing bothers him. He's my best friend, after you of course, my true-blue tennis shoe, my darling little pork chop, my sly secret agent, my bindle-doodle-hamster-queen, WHAT? All right, I'm going off the deep end, time to sign off. 'Member when we used to call each other "You big fat bucket full of water"? Thank God for being weird. Can you come over Saturday morning?

Love,
Bean

P.S. You SHOULD send Mick Jones a flower with a poem! He'll never know it was you. Do it, do it! I'll buy one for Enrique on Monday if you buy one for Mick.

Writing Notes for Flower Cards

Flower Card Note (Rejects):

Dear Enrique,
Keep up the excellent schoolwork.
Stay cute,
Bob Williams, Esquire

Dear Enrique,
I admire your ear. I also like the rest of you. You are
an adorable nugget of a boy.
I was wondering what you had planned for the rest
of your life and if perhaps I could join you.
Love, Your Mystery Woman
P.S. Please come to my midnight abode.

Dear Enrique,
How much pork could a pork chop chop
If a pork chop could chop pork?
Sincerely,
A.M.

Dear Enrique,
I have dreamed of your ear for many moons. The
way the skin around your eye crinkles when you look

into the microscope is like tiny rays of sunlight danc-
ing on my heart.
Dance little rays of light, dance!
Love,
The lover of your ear

Dear Enrique,
If you were a microscope, I would be your petri dish.
If you were a pork chop, I would be your applesauce.
If you were a flower, I would be a bee.
If you were an ear, I would be a Q-tip.
Sincerely,
Mrs. Midnight Abode

Dear Enrique,
Since we are in the midst of our painful adolescence,
I cannot reveal my true identity. It also turns out
I am an international spy & that is another reason I
cannot reveal my identity. I am sorry to send you a
flower anonymously, but know this: I love your ear
and if circumstances were different, I would invite
you to a midnight abode for a secret rendezvous.
Sincerely,
Agent Pork Chop

Flower-Card Notes (Keepers):

Enrique,
You are a charming little pork chop.
Sincerely,
A Secret Admirer

Dear Mick Jones,
You are a boy to whom all the girls flock
They perch like birds upon the hope
*   you will look their way.*
Will you give them a crumb, a smile a glance
If they wear the right dress will you ask them to
*   dance?*
Sitting and preening ignoring the sky
Why do girls forget they can fly?

~~~~~~

2

Flower Day

Cisco,

Oh blu blu blu bluub I'm a bundle of blubbering, bumbling nerves. Hows about you, my little true blue? The flowers are coming the flowers are coming the flowers are coming. Oh caca. In a little over an hour. I'm SO GLAD WE DECIDED TO DO OUR UNDERCOVER HOO-HAA. If I didn't get any flowers, I think I'd have to go home. Thank God I have you as my undercover buddy-butt.

My undercover buddy-butt.

Buddy-butt.

Can you tell I'm nervous?

I love Mrs. Pearson. I love drama production. I wish you liked drama. It's totally my favorite class. The fall production is *Joseph and the Technicolor Dreamcoat*. Auditions are in two weeks. I'm DEFINITELY gonna try out. Woah! Woah there, Horsey! Maybe it'll help my shyness. Or it's possible I'll just faint or even die during the audition. If I'm dead I DEFINITELY won't be shy anymore, eh? You should try out too. Please. I know you don't like drama, but you're the best dancer and you can definitely sing. Remember all the times we've done musical numbers in my rumpus room for Nelson or Emmett? Well, it's not that different! It can be part of our mission to be less shy and meet some boys. Oh, you have to—it's an excellent plan, in fact it's an ORDER, Agent number 88. I received our special encrypted, high-tech computer-chip command instructional message this morning in one of the nooks of my English muffin. So you have to try out—we've been given a mission straight from the top, from the head honcho, the Big Head Cheese. What's a honcho? Gotta go get an ice cream sandwich to calm my nerves.

OK, I'm back. THE TIME OF FLOWER DELIVERY IS IN UNDER AN HOUR! It's my free period; I'm supposed to be writing an essay. But I'm too fintatilated! (NEW WORD! Read it and weep!) Bye, Buddy-butt! Lunch in the usual spot, OK?

Bean

ADDENDUM: P.S. Can't write much science now but seem to have gotten a flower from Sean Higgins! Weirdness! It just says "Hi Annie, From Sean H." All flowers have been delivered. I got eight. Adolescent humiliation temporarily at bay. Show you at lunch. Can't write more—have Enrique's ear to gaze at/lab assignment. Mr. Peterson hates flower interruptus! Flirting practice this weekend? Sat. at my house? Eat this note.

Dear Bean,

Well, we survived Flower Day. And no one got even a whiff of our plan—mwa-ha-ha! MWA-HA-HA-HAAA! (evil-sounding laugh) Excellent job, Agent 66, excellent job. AND we both got some REAL flowers besides the ones we sent each other. Although, of course, I liked yours the best. You got one from Sean Higgins! Do you like him? I feel a little bad . . . Margaret P. got me one and I didn't get her one—just you and the bird man. I've no idea who that scribbly one is from; it's very mysterious—it's a good thing I'm an international spy with a finger-printing kit in my locker!

OK, we're on for Saturday flirting practice at your house—but we have to *swear* to secrecy, OK? We can't risk a leak of this magnitude or our whole undercover mission and our social lives will be TOTALLY blown to bits. Ugh, when will the bell ring?

I wonder what the bird man thought of his poem.

See you oh-so-shortly,
Cisco Nabisco

Cisco,

    I don't know Sean very well, but I do like his face and his hair! Which means I guess I like his whole head! The rest of him isn't so bad either! Let's say I'm *intrigued* by Sean. It'll be good to have flirting practice this weekend so that maybe I can get up the courage to talk to him! Why, *why* am I so shy?

Bean

~~~~~~

Izzy (Cisco)'s Journal

Flower Day was today and I got seven—five from Annie-Bean (as planned), one from Margaret Pope, and one mysterious flower. It had a scribble like this *Ʃʋɯ⌐*. Annie got eight: five from me, one from Sean, and two from girls in drama. I have this nervous feeling my scribble might be from Enrique Alvarez because during History, he asked me if I got any interesting flowers, and I just blushed and said, "Sure," and he said, "Any secret admirers?" and I just shrugged, and then he goes, "Secret admirers with *bad hand-writing*?" So . . . it seems like the scribbly one may be from him, which would be a **disaster** 'cause Annie likes him so much. Shoot, shoot, shoot. I mean, I kind of hope it's from him but equally hope it's not. She sent him one and always talks about his ear and stuff. He sits behind me in History class and has taken to yanking on my hair now and again and then when I turn around he tries to whistle and look away, but he always starts to laugh and then he can't whistle cause his lips won't stay pursed up in whistling mode. He's kinda cute, and if Annie didn't like him, I might just a little bit. I don't know. I think he's trying to flirt with me. I definitely cannot practice flirting back with him 'cause Annie likes him. Plus the fact that he sits behind me makes it even harder 'cause I'd have to turn all the way around and then I wouldn't know what to do—I'd just stare at him blankly, maybe drool a little.

I wish I lived in Jane Austen's time—I wish I wish I wish—when the guy would ask you to take a turn around the room. And he'd take your arm and you'd glide around the periphery of the room in your beautiful long gown and have a chat. Our heads would be inclined but never touching as we had an intimate tête-à-tête. He wouldn't just pull your hair and whistle and expect you to come up with something interesting to say. And he'd turn the pages for you as you sat prettily playing the piano. And he'd be enraptured by your gleaming ivory bosom, coyly nestled in your décolletage . . . and the softly straying, whisping tendrils of hair that swayed gently as you played a poignantly sweet piece of music that told of the longing about which neither of you could speak. Oh brother. I was born in the wrong time. My mom squeals (yes, literally squeals) when she's looking at *People* magazine and she sees cute hair or clothes. Sometimes I wonder which one of us is the teenager. She keeps showing me pictures of Ashley Simpson's hair and asking if I want to get my hair cut at Yosh. I think my Mom is afraid I'm not hip enough. I don't want to go to Yosh. I like my hair long, straight, and simple.

~~~~~~

Flirt Club Meeting One

Flirt Club Members: Annie-Bean (Secretary and Scribe) and Izzy (Founding Member Extraordinaire)

Rules of Flirt Club:

> Number one rule of Flirt Club: Never, EVER talk about Flirt Club.
> Number two rule of Flirt Club: Never, EVER talk about Flirt Club.
> Number three rule of Flirt Club: Never, EVER tell a soul about Flirt Club.

Minutes:

Flirting techniques I have observed Jeannie Mateo using on Scott Broderson:

1. She flips her hair a lot (this is a good technique for people with silky hair, e.g., Izzy—not so good for my already haywire curls. The last thing my hair needs is more activity.).
2. She bites the end of her pencil and looks at Scott with mischief in her eyes, like she knows a good secret—then he goes, "What?

WHAT?!" and she just shakes her head like he's a naughty boy.

3. She asks him questions about ANYTHING (and I mean anything . . . like, "Why do you think they made pencils yellow?").

4. She listens to his answers with wide eyes (and she sort of looks up at him from under her lashes).

5. She laughs and giggles A LOT, like whatever he says is witty.

6. She smacks him (not hard, and usually on the back of his head—I can tell he likes it).

7. She throws things at him (usually crumpled-up paper).

~~~~~~

Upon reflection, Izzy and I have decided that although we're willing to try the above-outlined techniques, we're pretty sure they're not really our style, especially playing dumb, *bleck*! Although I personally am not beyond lightly cuffing (Izzy's word) or throwing crumpled-up paper or whatnot at a Designated Target (aka cute boy). And Izzy's hair *is* fabulous when tossed about. I note for the record, though, that Izzy hates tossing her hair about "like a show pony," and although I offered to toss her hair about FOR her in the presence of attractive members of the opposite sex, she declined politely yet firmly.

OTHER FLIRTING IDEAS GENERATED DURING
"BRAINSTORMING SESSION" THAT ARE
PERHAPS MORE APPROPRIATE FOR
THE CURRENT MEMBERS
OF FLIRT CLUB:

8. If a guy looks at you, try to look back instead of immediately looking away. (WE AGREE THIS IS A VERY IMPORTANT BABY STEP AND A BASIC CHALLENGE WE FIND DIFFICULT, BUT WE HAVE AGREED TO WORK ON!!!)

9. If a guy looks at you and you are able to keep looking, try to go for a smile if you think he's cute.

10. Practice being friendly and conversational with people you don't know very well, even if they aren't people you want to flirt with. Practice, practice, practice.

11. If you have a question about something (a real one, not a dumb Jeannie-Mateo-type question), try to ask a cute boy.

POSSIBLE CONVERSATION STARTERS IN THE
INTEREST OF BEING FRIENDLY & HOPEFULLY
ONE DAY FLIRTATIOUS:

☆ What did you do last night?

☆ What did you do this weekend? (What are
you doing this weekend?)

☆ Ask about current activity or immediate
environment (e.g., Did you get the homework? What are you drawing? Did it hurt
when you got your nose pierced? Do you
always take the bus? ETC.!)

~~~~~~

(THESE WERE HARD TO COME UP WITH!!!!)
ARE WE BIG OL' DORKS? YEP!!!!!!!!!!!!!!!!!!!!!!!!!!!!!!!!!!
!!
!!!

This should be called "Dork Club"! or "Cisco and the
Bean's School for Ever-Expanding Dorkdom." Oh well, **A for
effort!!!!!!!!!!!!!!!!!!!!!!!!!!!!!!!!!!**

**Practice session (Every meeting of Flirt Club must
commence/conclude with a practice session!)**
We practiced on my cat, Nelson. My session went something
like this:

27

I sit near Nelson with my arms relaxed in my lap after being instructed by Izzy not to always have my arms crossed over my chest and be totally hunched over (body language is important!), which is something I do all the time.

"So, Nelson, how's your weekend going?"

Flick of Nelson's pretty green eyes.

"Oh, really? I didn't know you played soccer . . . So, how's your team doing?"

Nelson stretched and yawned.

"Oh cool, well, that's great." Etc., etc. as Nelson and I discuss soccer, the challenges of muddy cleats, etc . . .

Izzy's session with Nelson:

"Hi Nelson, I really like your collar. Is that new?" (Compliments are good.)

Nelson looks at Izzy with benign, slightly bored expression.

"Wow, from your grandfather? How long has it been in the family?"

Nelson blinks.

"That's amazing. I have a pair of shoes from the 1920s that used to be my grandmother's. I may wear them to the Halloween Dance." Etc., etc. as Izzy finds out what Nelson is going to be for Halloween and if he's going to the dance, leaving ample opportunity in the conversation for him to invite her as a date! Which he fails to do because he's a cat!

Due to the soft, adorable nature of our practice subject, we both ended our practice session scritching and scratching

Nelson and burying our faces in his tummy because he's
SUCH A SOFT LOVE PUDDLE!

Note: NOT what we would do with an ADT (Actual Designated Target) (AKA boy)!

Izzy wrote a very short poem for our darling boyfriend,
Nelson the Cat:
It's called

"King of My Heart"
Hello His Orangeness
His Highness
His fat Pumpkin-Pieness

Hello His Fuzziness
His Plumpness
His soft-footed, graceful, Never-go-bumpness

Izzy rocks! Practicing with Nelson was a little too easy, so we
made ourselves walk down the street and start a conversation
with a real person. The only real person we encountered on our
mission was Mrs. Healy (an oldish lady) digging in her garden.
We stood awkwardly on the sidewalk for a few minutes and
then we asked her about her plants and gardening gloves and
stuff. It was kind of embarrassing and then it was actually kind
of nice. She told us all about her "baby's tears" ground cover, its
"tenuous nature," its "delicacy." It's actually very pretty. And

then she had us popping her fuchsia flower buds. She said, "They were ready for popping."

In Conclusion/Things we have learned at Flirt Club:

1. Smiling, questions/showing interest are a good start. (The worst thing that can happen is that someone feels cared about.)
2. Hair flipping is not a good approach for either of us.
3. I am considering throwing things (that don't hurt) at an ADT (Actual Designated Target).
4. Fuchsia buds are super fun to pop.
5. Baby's tears is delicate and needs moisture and shade.

And thus concludes the first meeting of Flirt Club.

3

Beyond Popping Fuchsias

Dear Cisco,

It's my free period and I'm sitting in Center Quad. Woooweee. Or other sounds that connote relief. I love this time of year when the air starts to crispen right up (made-up word alert). Well, well, well . . . some interesting developments have developed since Flower Day, and I don't think they're just in my imagination. Development number 1—Sean Higgins is totally acting weird around me. I think he's embarrassed he sent me a flower. He doesn't chat with me anymore during English. He's acting awkward. He doesn't look at me hardly at all anymore. He smiled at me once today, but it was one of those stiff, baring-teeth-like-a-wild-animal smiles. Is it possible that cute boys are shy too? I wish I could show him that I think he's cute and nice & that I was glad for his flower, but I'm shy. It's been over a week since I received it, and I haven't even said thank you. Good Gump, didn't my mother teach me any manners?

31

I HAVE to. But him being shy is making me even MORE shy, which is making HIM more shy, etc.! It's awful . . . pretty soon we'll both be blubbering idiots around each other or maybe even MUTE idiots, hiding under our desks, squeezing our eyes shut, and rocking.

I have to take the horse by the reins. Grab the alligator by the tail, squeeze the monkey by the balls. WHAT? No, I'm joshing, but I do have to IMPLEMENT our mission, Number 88, and soon!

Development number 2: Is really a lack of a development, actually. Enrique is acting totally normal around me. Very relaxed, very casual. He has no idea that I am his little flower-sending gnome. None. In one way I'm relieved, but in another way I'm disappointed. I don't know—I guess I had some tucked away hope that he'd intuitively KNOW I was the sender and sweep me off my feet at our lab station and yell, "MY LITTLE PORK CHOP!! I'VE BEEN WAITING ALL MY LIFE FOR THIS MOMENT!" AND THEN SWEEP OUR MICRO-SCOPE, BINDERS, ETC. TO THE FLOOR, HOIST ME UP ON OUR LAB TABLE AND PRESS HIS BEAUTI-FUL EAR TO MY CHEEK PASSIONATELY. Should I have signed my name? No, I just can't fathom it, the embarrass-ment! That Jeannie Mateo is something else! She has no shy-ness, none whatsoever! She's all boldness. She's boldness dipped in brazenness sprinkled with chutzpah! I saw her walk up to JOEY CACCIONE (!!!!) with a lollipop in her mouth and go,

32

all coy and playful, "So, are you gonna invite me to the Halloween dance or what?" and he just goes, "Are you gonna give me that lollipop or what?" and SHE DOES! She PULLS IT OUT OF HER OWN MOUTH and HOLDS IT IN HIS MOUTH WHILE HE SUCKS ON IT!

And then I think of us popping Mrs. Healy's fuchsia bushes and I have to admit I feel a little discouraged.

I *will* smile at Sean Higgins tomorrow, I *will*.

Love,
Bean

Bean,

Agent #66, you must complete your assignment (smile at S.H.) before the end of the week. He's probably thinking you don't like him, poor guy. I know for a fact that other girls like him, so you have to make a move. I heard Madison Geller and Alanna Markley talking in the snack bar line about how cute he is and wondering if he has a girlfriend, etc. So, the popular girls have their eyes on him—DO something.

I have absolutely no developments to report. I've only seen Mick Jones a couple times in the hall and he doesn't even look at me. But thank God . . . I would die if he knew I sent that poem.

OK, I do have *one* development to report—and don't scream when you read this, BUT—I will try out for *Joseph* with you. It's mostly singing and dancing, right? Not as much acting? I like to sing and dance—mostly when I'm in the shower or home in the living room. BUT it will be good for the mission, and plus if I don't do it I'll never see you after school.

Come over this weekend and let's pretend we're in *A Chorus Line* like we used to in 6th grade. And, of course, let's have another meeting of Flirt Club. Let's go to Mayfield Mall so we can practice on an ADT. OK? Versus on someone who's a cat or a little old lady, OK?

Love, your friend always,
Cisco-co-puff

Dear Cisco,
Ahhhh! Yay! Yippee! You're trying out for *Joseph*! The auditions are October 6, which is coming up soon—yikes! And, yes! We're on for this weekend, Flirt Club and doing Broadway musicals in your living room. Do you still have *Jesus Christ Superstar*? "I don't know how to love him, what to do, how to move him . . ." You said it Sister Mary Magdalene. I DON'T know how to love him. (*Him* being Sean H., not J.C.) THAT IS MY THEME SONG.

GOD SAVE US FROM OUR OWN DRAMA-GEEK TENDENCIES!!

Oh brother, WHAT a fiasco at lunch.

OK, you have to admit that I tried, right? I TRIED to implement one of our techniques.

I said I was going to try throwing something at an ADT and I did. If Sean had been sitting at the table next to ours instead of three tables over, I probably could have pulled it off. Or if I had better aim. Poor Danny Rosenberg. What does he think of us? Him and Glenn Gould just happened to be in the line of fire. Shoot, I should have stopped after the first French fry hit Danny's head. But I had to try again and probably I shouldn't have used that rubbery hamburger bun. At least it didn't have ketchup or mustard on it. I can't believe I hit Danny twice right in the back of the head like that. Maybe I do have good aim. And if you hadn't laughed so hard that your head almost fell off, he would never have known it was us. And *then* he picks up the bun, walks over, and carefully places it on my knee and says, "Um, I think you misplaced a portion of your meal." I almost died! At least he wasn't mad.

Why? Why can't I just walk up to Sean and go, "Thanks for the flower. Hey, are you going to the Halloween dance?" or "Thanks for the flower. Are you on the swim team? 'Cause your hair is so sparkly it's like spun gold and brings to mind one of God's highest and most good-looking angels." NOT! Me and my errant buns. I'm a rogue bun thrower. The following is to be sung to the tune of Pat Benatar's "Heart Breaker":

35

I'm a bun thrower
Food flinger, fry slinger
Don't you mess around with me!
I'm a bun thrower
Food flinger, fry slinger
Don't you mess around—no, no, no!

I'm going to try to throw something at him during English. I'll have a better shot. Did you see Mia Shepard walk up to him at lunch? You're right, the popular girls ARE ON THE MOVE—I HAVE TO ACT FAST. I'll leave you with this thought:

"He's a man, (well, not quite) *he's just a man* (a man-child, really). *And I've had so many men before* (Um . . . actually more like none). *In very many ways. He's just one more."*

Love,
Bean Bean the Magical Fruit

P.S. OK, I agree, REAL ADTs this weekend—no cats, no fuchsia popping for Mrs. Healy.

P.P.S. Did you know that I, like baby's tears, am delicate? That I need plenty of moisture? (I really do or my poo won't come out. Please feed this note to your dog.)

Dear Bean,

Did you know that *I* am like a fuchsia bud in that I am a wallflower who hangs her head and stares at the ground whenever boys are around.

Love,
Cisco

Dear Cisco:

Gotta write quick. I did it—threw a crumpled piece of paper at Sean. (I was shaking.) He looked around and I gave him a big red-faced smile that I'm sure looked like a seizure, and he raised his eyebrows all cool and then winked.

Mlaaaa! I flirted! In a spastic kind of way. He winked.

Is he a winker?

I don't know what to do with that.

In the timeless words of Mary in *Jesus Christ Superstar,* "Should I scream and shout, Should I speak of love, let my feelings out?"

~Bean

~~~~~~

Izzy (Cisco)'s Journal

Well, Enrique Alvarez DID send me that scribbly flower. All week he's been really friendly, talking to me in History class so much that finally Mr. Poff threatened to move him and told him "to please conduct his personal business outside the classroom." And the boys go OOOOOooo. That was so embarrassing I thought I'd shrivel. But then Enrique started passing me notes. The first one said, "Did you like the flower I sent you?" And he signed it in the same scribbly letters that were on the card. So it was definitely from him. I wrote back, "Yes, thanks!"

Ah, I feel so weird . . . I haven't told Annie-Bean 'cause it may hurt her feelings and I sort of like him but I wouldn't do ANYTHING if it would hurt her. I'm sort of hoping that something will happen with her and Sean Higgins and then I could tell her about Enrique without it being weird. Oh lord, I don't know. She'll wonder why I didn't tell her before.

Then today Enrique sent me a note saying, "You are a mermaid." And I sent him back a note that said, "More like a merblob." See, I don't want to be mean & ignore him, but I don't want to flirt back. THEN he sent me a more obvious one saying, "I'm losing my heart in your long black treeses." I think he meant "tresses," so I wrote, "My TREESES? What trees?" trying to be funny, but then he didn't write back and I felt bad and worried that I'd hurt his feelings. But then when the bell rang, he grabbed my hair (gently) and put his face near mine and said, "*Tresses,* your long black *tresses,*" so close to my ear it made my head tingle. And then he looked me right in the eye. Neither of us looked away, and I wanted to die but in a good way. CRAPPPP. I keep thinking about his eyes and his hand full of my hair.

THAT was a good flirting technique. I don't know what to do. The bummer is I can't talk to Annie about any of this.

~~~~~~~~~~~~~~~~~~~~~~~~~~~~~~~~~~~~~

Flirt Club Minutes: Official Meeting Number Two

Flirt Club Members: Annie the Bean (Secretary and Scribe) and Izzy the Cisco (Member of the Cabinet)

> Flirt Club Rule Number One: Don't talk about Flirt Club to anyone in the known universe.
> Flirt Club Rule Number Two: Don't talk about . . . OK, we get the picture.

Review of flirting techniques that we tried this week:
Annie tried throwing things at Sean Higgins. The food throwing was DISASTROUS. The paper throwing and goofy smile thereafter was a success and procured a WINK!

Though the question arises: is Sean Higgins turning into a player? (Though neither of us knows exactly what a player is, we think it may include WINKING AT THE LADIES.)

Izzy tried a couple of times to catch Mick Jones's eye in the hallway, but according to her, he looked right through her or past her or next to her—basically anywhere but at her. Apparently he does not know she exists. Conclusion: Izzy needs a more reasonable ADT.

Well, we made a teeny bit of progress this week.

Neither of us have any new flirting techniques to report.

STRIKE THAT! Izzy suggested one new flirting technique: Gentle hair pulling. (Stress on the gentle—we don't want to start any schoolyard brawls.)

(I thought this was a little grade-school-esque, along the lines of snapping girls' bras, but Izzy disagreed.)

Since we didn't have a lot of new ideas this week, we reviewed last week's minutes and now we're off to Mayfield Mall to practice on ADTs, aka BOYS.

We'll be back (said like the Terminator).

Notes on practice session:

Mission accomplished! We went to the pet store at the mall and hung out there. We saw two guys who were sort of cute and interesting standing in front of the hamsters. I pushed Izzy (who was frozen like a Popsicle!) toward them, and we all stood there slightly awkwardly, just staring at this immense tubular hamster playground. Well, it turned out that one of the guys was trying to pick a hamster as a present for his little sister. I was eavesdropping and I just (oh so boldly, I might add!) go, "How old is your sister?" and he goes, "Nine." And then I told him he should get one of the extra fluffy ones 'cause that's what I would have wanted as a young girl. And then we all talked a little bit about how the long-haired ones looked glamorous, like rock-star hamsters or something, and then Izzy said that the fluffy round ones look kind of like cat toys, which made everyone laugh (clever, clever girl!) though she wasn't trying to be funny. Then there was an awkward silence and the other guy goes, "So, are you girls in the market for a hamster?" And I turned to Izzy 'cause I kind of froze, and she goes, "Weeellll, I've been considering it, yes, I've been considering acquiring a hamster." God bless her lying soul! (Just a little white one, of course, all for the sake of the mission!) And then we all nodded at each other a lot, and I go, "Well, bye, good luck with your purchase!" That was a little dorky, but we did it! We struck up a conversation with boys! I mean my palms were drenched while it was happening, but afterward I felt like I had successfully manned a lunar mission! Woo-hoo! They were nice too, and easy to practice on.

In Conclusion/Things we have learned at Flirt Club:
1. Throwing things (not bricks or chairs) at an ADT can actually work, BUT
2. Don't throw hamburger buns at Danny Rosenberg. NO MORE THROWING FOOD!
3. Striking up a conversation is an excellent option. (THOUGH IT CAN INDUCE SWEAT!)
4. Fluffy hamsters make excellent cat toys.

Progress is upon us!

And thus concludes Flirt Club meeting number 2.

4
Audition Day

Dear Cisco,

Does too much popcorn make your poo hard and unforgiving? I am having some . . . *um* . . . trouble. Let's just say, Elvis has NOT left the building!

Love,
Bean

Bean,

Uh-oh! Did I feed you too much popcorn last night? I'm sorry to hear about "Elvis." Maybe it's audition nerves. I'm *totally* nervous. Nervo spazo. Nervoid. Devoid of calm.

Love,
Cisco

Dear Cisco,

I'm sure it's the audition nerves and not your popcorn that's giving me bowel difficulties . . . last year, around opening night of *The Music Man,* Elvis didn't leave the building for three whole days! Having popcorn and watching DVDs last night was actually a good distraction. BUT NOW THERE'S NO ESCAPING IT!!! Auditions are here auditions are here auditionjsnsthb aer g herereedkld. (I'm trying to give the impression of the blithering idiot that I am.) My stomach is a pit of writhing vipers. My palms are sweating in a continuous and annoying manner.

> *"Will you touch, will you mend me, Christ?*
> *Will you kiss, you can cure me, Christ?"*

I wish someone would kiss me . . . not necessarily our Lord and Savior, but I've never been kissed by a boy.

Sigh . . .

Never been kissed . . .

Sigh . . .

Except when Matthew Bellisari used to pin me to the mural wall and squish his mouth on mine in 1st grade. Once he even sucked on my chin for a moment. Not too romantic. Quite GROSS, in fact. That was so fun this weekend!! Even if we never get boyfriends, we will always be able to have fun, fun, FUN because we'll have each other. Ahhhh! Speaking of getting boyfriends, guess who's an item?? Jeannie Mateo and Joey Caccione! She is masterful! And coiffed, of course! I'M SO GLAD YOU'RE AUDITIONING TOO! There are not a lot of big parts for girls in this show, but Mrs. P. said she might cast some girls as the brothers or have more than one narrator because there are so many girls in drama. I'd love to be a brother. I don't want to be a wife, really. I bet Andrew Pease will be Joseph. How can someone that skinny belt it out like that? It's amazing. OK, Mrs. Kelly is here, class is starting, gotta go.

Love,
Bean

P.S. Let's warm up our voices in the bathroom or down by the field during lunch, OK?

Bean,

I'm so nervous I feel a little sick. Why? Why did I decide to do this? I can't act. Writing you is the only thing that helps. Remember when your folks took us to see *Jesus Christ Superstar* in 6th grade? And 'member how Jesus had all that chest hair? Why did they put him in that white spandex V-neck thing anyway? A simple robe would have been best. That chest hair was so distracting. AND you could see it all bumpy and curly under the white spandex. Eww. Somehow I think of Jesus as someone with a smooth chest, not a virile, hairy guy. And 'member how Pontius Pilate kept spraying spittle when he sang? It was so noticeable in the stage lights, like a fine, misted rain. Well, my 7th-grade choir teacher, Mr. Libratore, is the music director for *Joseph*, so *that's* good 'cause I'll be less nervous at the audition. Plus he knows I can sing OK, so he'll know it's just nerves if I sound like a rusted nail being pounded into a rotted piece of wood or a cat whose tail is being stepped on or an old man who's been smoking cigars all night.

OK, let's go down by the field at lunch & practice. I know that's where the stoners go, but I DON'T want to be all "La la la la la la!" in the bathroom. Even if we hid in stalls. Actually that would be funny to just sit in separate stalls and sing. That would freak people out. Like, remember the time we hid in those big crates with Christmas trees in them at the Christmas tree lot and sang in opera voices and shook the trees. That was awesome. Let's think of a replacement word for "awesome." "Awesome" is not awesome. It's all dried up, it's seen better days. It's not for us.

Love,
Cisco

Cisco,

Replacements for "awesome":

crispy ("Woah, that is so crispy!")
rawsome

45

confabuloso

naird ("Like, that's totally naird, dude.")

flambambishmentato

That's my favorite. Cisco, your voice sounded totally flam-bambishmentato at lunch. Last year Jing-Wei the choreographer taught us a dance combo in advance of the auditions so we had time to practice, but then some people started a political movement called "Down With Advanced Learning of Choreography!" because some people had free periods and more time to practice (like yours truly) and some people didn't, so *some* people were better prepared (like yours truly). Some people! Actually, I understand their point. It's just I'm a slow study when it comes to dance steps, unlike you, Goddess of All Dance Forms. I have to go . . . we're supposed to be reading about the Constitutional Convention though I'm *way* too nervous to concentrate! I'll go ask to use the restroom and go put this in your locker. I hope I don't stumble around and land in a pool of my own nervous sweat.

"Will you touch, will you mend me, Christ?" I'm a broken record!

OK, I'll see you in the auditorium after school. You're going to do great because you're totally naird, my friend, totally naird.

Love,
Bean

P.S. Oh my Gump, I totally remember Pontius Pilate spitting up the place! That was hysterical! Say it, don't spray it, OK, Pontius? Why is no one named Pontius anymore?

Dearest Bean,

I say we bring back the name Pontius. I'll agree to name my first child (regardless of its sex) Pontius if you do. And then Pontius and Pontius can have playdates. I'm done with the test we took today. And I'm free, free as a bird now (and this bird will never change). Well, at least I'm free to sit at my small desk in total silence and barely move. Now there's freedom for you. Actually my mind is free, free to commune with you and THAT'S ALL I NEED! (big dramatic swell of poignant Hollywood music).

I don't want to be a brother or a narrator. So I guess that leaves the chorus or a wife. The chorus would be perfect, not too much attention or responsibility, not too nerve-wracking. But still lots of scenes. I hope I'm not a farm animal. Mr. Libratore said they were thinking of busing some elementary kids in to be in the farm animal scene. That sounds good. Small children are not embarrassed to act like sheep and cows and pigs—it would be fun for them versus the deeply psychologically damaging humiliation it would be for us.

I'll probably see you before you read this, but I'm always

talking to you in my head anyway so I may as well write it down!

Love,
Cisco

P.S. YOUR voice sounded totally confabulouso at lunch—you're gonna do great! I bet you get a big part.

~~~~~~

Izzy (Cisco)'s Journal ~ Audition Day

The auditions went pretty good. My nerves were pretty much under control until I had to read a monologue from *Man-in-the-Moon Marigolds* and my hands were actually shaking—I'm afraid everyone in the audience could see the paper shaking. But the dancing and singing went well. Jing-Wei, the choreographer, moved me up to the front row after we learned the combination, so I think that was a good sign. The singing was fine—really short 'cause Mr. Libratore said he was very familiar with my voice from choir last year. Mrs. Pearson said the cast list goes up on Friday. There were a lot of talented kids trying out—PLENTY of boys—so I don't think Mrs. P. will need to use girls for the brothers, which is too bad for Annie 'cause she wanted to be a brother. I hope she gets Potiphar's wife. Michael Maddix tried out! I can't believe it. He hasn't done any drama since 6th grade—I thought he was too cool for drama now. AND he was awesome; I mean, he was blamfambishmentato.

I don't know what to do about Enrique. He still grabs my hair and talks to me on the way out of class almost every day. I'm nice in an awkward, totally shy way, but not flirty—even if I had a clue how to flirt, I never would when Annie-Bean likes him so much. Flup, he's so cute though. Maybe something will develop with Annie and Sean Higgins and then I can talk to Annie about the Enrique thing. I don't know, though, I think Sean is enjoying his growth spurt, new manliness (and thus the attention he's getting from girls—I heard Mia S. talking about him again; she said he was "a hottie"!). It seems like one of those totally bold popular girls may snap him up. That would be sad for Annie. And Sean would accomplish the impossible—break the sound barrier and enter the popular group. THIS IS SOMETHING I WOULD NEVER ADMIT TO ANYONE (not even Annie), but I probably would be in the popular group if I *could,* wouldn't I? I act like I don't really care about that sort of thing, but I do. Sometimes. It's a little like being famous. One thing I've noticed, too, is that the popular girls and boys aren't afraid to talk to the opposite sex. They all eat lunch together and SEEM like they're having such a good time. All that screeching and stuff. Good night sweet diary.

CAST LIST FOR *JOSEPH AND THE AMAZING TECHNICOLOR DREAMCOAT*

Joseph: Michael Maddix

Narrator: Katie Chethik

Pharaoh: Eric Burkhart

Jacob/Potiphar: Andrew Pease

Brothers: Alex Boerum

Walter Drake

Chris Collins

Billy Carlson

Steve Nomoki

Holden McCabe

Courtney Reynolds

WIVES:

Potiphar's Wife: Eva Stark

Beth Quinlin

Mary Matatta

Samantha Francisco

Rachel Lordes

Deborah Wagstaff

Julia Parks

Beth Canody

CORN, ETC.:

Myrna Mendez

Lisa Newcomb

Isabelle Mercer-Crow

Annie Myers

Ariane Neville

FARM ANIMALS: (OF FAIRMEADOW
ELEMENTARY)

Christopher Ray

Jocelyn Turner

Kimberly Caldwell

Cisco,

Although traditionally when I'm in mourning I don't write notes during free period (traditionally I howl, thrash about, and rend my garments in Center Quad), I am making an exception because I believe that writing you will help me get through this very difficult time of life.

CORN????

We're flupping CORN??? Dancing, singing CORN?

What the FLUP???

This sucks so much that my vacuum cleaner is jealous of its sucking power.

This sucks so much that all the leeches in the world have given up their calling (of sucking) because they are disheartened by the superior suckage of this situation.

This sucks so much that my dad's Shop-Vac is a weak little kitten in comparison.

This sucks so much that vampires around the world are clinking their crystal goblets full of blood together, celebrating this new and breathtakingly powerful form of SUCKING!

Oh Cisco, Cisco, Cisco, in the timeless words of Mary Magdalene in *Jesus Christ Superstar*—*"What's it all about?"* Flup this. We're going to be rehearsing four afternoons a week and doing twelve shows, INCLUDING WEEKEND NIGHTS, to star as a fantabulous piece of corn. Flup.

I'm doing some serious thinking about the value of this sort of debacle. Some serious rethinking. And then some more thinking and then again some rethinking. BUT! I can't be a big diva-pants, a big pouty poop-in-my-diaper baby and be like, *"Corn?? Well, I Quit! That'll teach you to cast me as a common crop vegetable!"* Suddenly I'm blanking—is corn a vegetable? It's not a fruit or a nightshade, it MUST be a vegetable. ANY-HOO, I can't be all fussy like that and remain in good standing with Mrs. P. But ... CORN??? I put my time in last year doing costumes for *Bye Bye Birdie* and being in the chorus for *The Music Man*. I thought I'd be promoted instead of *demoted to a singing vegetable!* This is a downfall of unfathomable proportions. I know I'm being a drama queen. I can't help it, that's my nature. Flup. Well, I guess I'll just have to get over myself. Ugh. Bite the bullet and stretch, stretch my acting capabilities to encompass being a starchy husked vegetable.

I guess it's pulling myself up by the bootstrap time.

Here's a short story (very short): Once there were two girls named Cisco and the Bean. Life sometimes knocked them down. What with being wallflowers and oddballs and mostly invisible to boys and playing vegetables in the school play and all, they were always having to pick themselves up by the bootstraps. Always having to cheer themselves (and each other) up up up and away. They got good at it and their bootstraps got really long and stretched out from all that hoisting. But they were still upright. Mostly. Except when they had aspirations to be more than singing corn and those aspirations were mercilessly bitch-slapped down.

The End.

Sincerely,
Fumbling for My Bootstraps (aka, your loving Bean)

Beany Baby!
Oh, I know! Corn. I'm just glad I got in the show at all, but I can imagine how you must feel. I love you very much and I

just had to crunch up this note momentarily and hide it in my hand 'cause Mr. Sperry started strolling around the room, which he never does. Gots to be brief. Sorry for the wrinkly note. Anyhoo, you are a star in *my* sky always.

Love,
Cisco

5

Projectile Correspondence

~~~~~~

<u>Annie (Bean)'s Diary</u>

Well, even though I'm corn it's not as bad as I originally thought. We're in the chorus and although that includes being dancing, singing corn, it also includes being one of the pharaoh's dancing Egyptian handmaidens AND an "Adoring Girl" AND dancing, singing colors of the rainbow in the finale. So, we're in lots o' scenes. SO, that's not so bad. Why couldn't Mrs. P. have just put "Chorus" instead of "Corn" on the cast list? That was humiliating. God bless her soul, but was she trying to damage us psychologically? Does she remember being young? Doesn't she know how easy it is to wound the soul of a sensitive artistic type? (I, like baby's tears, am delicate and need moisture and shade.) Anyway, it'll be SO MUCH FUN to be with Izzy! And Myrna, Ariane, and Lisa from 7th-period drama too! Couldn't have asked for a better bunch of corn! And Mrs. P. explained we're not actually singing *pieces* of corn; we're singing *stalks* of corn. We'll have tassels on our heads poking out of pointy green hats. And thank God they're bussing the farm animals in from Fairmeadow Elementary. It would be far worse to be cast as "sheep #2" or "cow #4."

In further news I am so confused about Sean Higgins. OK, it's been over a week since "The Throwing of the Paper" that was followed by the infamous "Winking of His Eye" and not much has happened. I've managed to catch his eye a handful of times during class and two of those times he smiled at me and once I actually managed to smile back—not just squinch up my face nervously. I wish he didn't sit all the way across the room. I don't know, I was hoping for something a little more dramatic—like maybe him throwing something at *me,* or passing me a note or talking to me after class. I'm probably expecting him to do too much of the scary stuff... I mean, look at Jeannie Mateo. If she likes someone, she showers them with lollipops and giggles and constant attention and glimpses of her newly glossed, ever shiny lips while **simultaneously** giving off an aura of not really caring what they think. *How does she do that?* She's so twisty, she's like a Yogi of flirtation. If I think about it from Sean's point of view, he sent me a flower and I didn't even thank him. All I've done is pummel him with one measly wad of paper. I SHOULD HAVE WRITTEN SOMETHING ON THE PAPER! That shall be my next mission, if I choose to accept it. And, in fact, yes, I do, I choose to accept it! I'm worried that some of those popular girls may like him.

Izzy's heard them talking about him, and I've seen them circling like hawks. And who wouldn't—that shiny swimmer's hair on that golden brown skin, and I love his jacket. Sigh. What a hottie. AND a smarty. He doesn't live near the rich kids; he lives closer to us—someone said he lived on Sutherland.

Flirt Club this weekend. Maybe Myrna and Ariane and Lisa could come. A gathering of the corn. Right now, I'm a sleepy, sleepy corn.

Dear Cisco, aka Agent #88,

It's my free period so I am at my leisure to write to you, my darling, my cornstalk.

Well, OK, I'll say it: being corn in the chorus is not so bad. In fact, IT'S TOTALLY FUN.

Aren't Myrna and Lisa and Ariane nice? Our corn dance is a little boring, but I love the Egyptian scene—and Jing-Wei put us in the front row for the Egyptian AND the color dance. Woo-hoo and other celebratory sounds. Even though Thursday is a rehearsal for just the Brothers, do you wanna go watch again? I love hanging out in the theater even when we're not rehearsing. DRAMA GEEK ALERT. Woo-woo-woo (that's the sound of the geek siren.) And maybe Michael M. will be singing "Close Every Door." Flup he sounds (AND LOOKS) good. And we could sit in the audience and stare at him in dewy-eyed longing. Do you remember in 2nd grade when he was Winnie the Pooh in the class play and you were Tigger and I was Eeyore? 'Member how we used to bounce around the schoolyard being Tiggers for hours? Bouncing pouncing bouncing POUNCING, that's what Tiggers do best. Here's a thought—let's pounce on Michael Maddix today during rehearsal, eh? And say (with a big lisp of course), "That's what Tiggers do best!" How's that for a flirting technique? Pouncing on our prey? MWA-HA-HA-HAAAAaaaa!

OK, Agent #88, in other, more serious news—today is the day I carry out my assignment: to throw a piece of paper at Sean Higgins THAT HAS SOMETHING WRITTEN ON IT!! Darling, although I loved your idea to quote that Yeats poem about a fire burning in my head (a little flirtatious in a mysterious and slightly strange way), I'm afraid Sean Higgins wouldn't have a clue about it and may assume I am some sort of pyromaniac. Or on drugs! OR, if he does for some BIZARRE reason know it's "The Wandering Angus" by William Butler Yeats, will he think I'm referring to him as a man cow? Or likening *myself* to wayward cattle? Do you see the possible confusion that could ensue? I think I'll simplify matters and just write, "HI SEAN." OK, God-of-small-brave-but-immature-acts, give me courage to do this! God-of-all-arms-and-shy-limbs, give my arm the strength to throw my note! OK—I'll write more later, after English class, and let you know how my mission went.

Love,
Bean

ADDENDUM (It's positively dorky how much I love that word):

Enrique and I are done with our lab so I am free to write, which is good because I am bursting—I DID IT! I threw a note at my ADT! Oh it was disastrous! And glorious! OK, first about the disaster. Mrs. Kelly SAW me throw it (she must have eyes on the back of her well-coiffed head), and she asked Sean to bring the note to the front of the class. She opened it up and, of course, people were all "oooooo" and I was expiring on the spot—my face was redder than my hair IF that's possible. Mrs. Kelly slowly opened it and read it (not aloud, thank God) and handed it back to Sean. Then she goes, very quiet but deadly, "Annie Myers, you must be confused," and just looks at me. The class was TOTALLY SILENT at this point. I go, "Excuse me?" She goes, "Do you think this is a Physical Education class Miss Myers?" I shook my head (I could hardly breathe, much less talk. I was pretty much too embarrassed to be alive at this point). Then she goes, "Well, then, please stop practicing your *athletic skills*. English class is not a place for THROWING THINGS, INCLUDING PROJECTILE

CORRESPONDENCE." I go, "Sorry, Mrs. Kelly," although I was already dead of embarrassment and living in a hell realm of mortification. Of course there were the inevitable titters and chuckles as Sean walked back to his desk. BUT the one saving glory is that he winked at me as he sat down FOR ALL THE WORLD TO SEE! *Then* the other BIGGER saving glory is that on the way out of class as I was darting out the door like a rat drowned in the sweat of its own untimely demise, Sean grabbed my backpack and pulled me to him! He said, "I wanted to congratulate you on your athletic skills. That's a nice throwing arm you've got." And HE SQUEEZED MY UPPER ARM and *then* held out his hand for me to shake. So I wordlessly shook it and he passed me a crumpled note and walked away. It said, "HI ANNIE." So I have been through the fires of hellish mortification and I am cleansed and reborn unto a new world where Sean Higgins talked to me! And shook my hand. Let's have a Flirt Club Scrapbook/ Almanac where we display the spoils of our victories! This note from Sean is one for the Almanac! Though it was hard won, hard won indeed. I still get red thinking about it. I am *not* one to cause trouble in class! Jeez, you know me—I ain't NEVER misbehavin'! "Projectile correspondence" indeed!

So, you wanna hang in the auditorium today and watch rehearsals? Lisa's going to. She's gonna try to teach me how to knit. Do you know her darling little periwinkle hoody? SHE

KNITTED THAT. Did you know she makes a lot of her own clothes? She wants to be a designer.

Love,
Bean the Mortified

Dearest Bean,

I'm *so glad* you threw something at Sean—mission accomplished Agent 66. The organization is proud of your work, you shall be honored with a plaque that says:

> In Commemoration of Annie Meyers,
> Secret Agent Extraordinaire
> For Outstanding Achievement in the Field of Flirting
> Your sacrifice and dedication in the volatile arena of
> Paper Throwing will benefit generations to come.

I'll see you at the theater after school so we can stare (and drool) at Michael Maddix and the other boys as they rehearse! I love Lisa's clothes; she should *totally* be a designer.

Love,
Cisco

Dear Cisco,

Don't use my real name in notes! Don't worry, I ate the last one you sent me—no wonder my bowels give me so much trouble. Ha-ha, just kidding! I haven't eaten any paper since kindergarten, when I longed, and sometimes couldn't resist, to taste the construction paper to see what the different colors tasted like!

And thanks for the imaginary plaque!

See you at 3:30,
Bean (s on toast)

~~~~~~~~~~~~~~~~~~~~~~~~~~~~~

<u>Izzy (Cisco)'s Journal</u>

I am so annoyed. I can feel my age-old crush on Michael Maddix vaguely returning. I thought I'd finally let it go after we got to Wilbur and it became clear that he and I were ending up in different groups and we basically stopped socializing. I liked him for pretty much *all* of elementary school and nothing ever happened. I was wise enough to LET IT DROP. Especially since he's in the popular group and he's going out with Shelly Scott, who's got to be one of the cutest girls in school. Why is he suddenly interested in drama again? He sure can sing. For a whole year I almost forgot he existed, and now I think about his existence all the time! When he was working with Mr. Libratore today on his song it may have been my imagination but it seemed like he smiled at me a few times. Can you even see into the audience when you're on stage? I should test it out on Monday. He was probably just basking in the female attention.

Almost all the girls in the cast were watching the boys rehearse. Is that totally geeky? I mean we had no other reason to be there except to watch the boys. And hang out together. I LOVE BEING IN THE PLAY!!! We DID practice our choreography in the lobby after Mr. Libratore made us leave.

I CAN'T crush out on Michael again! It's such a waste of time. I'm like one of those old-fashioned war brides who loves one man her whole life and remains true to him. Except I was never married to Michael. Or was his girlfriend. Or have any indication that he is even aware of my existence anymore. Oh brother. I'm pathetic. BUT I do like Enrique a little bit, although that will probably never amount to anything due to the Annie factor and my shyness. Enrique asked if I was going to the Halloween dance (he just asked IF, not if I would go with him). I said I thought so.

Dear Cisco,

Who ever thought I would have such a good time being dancing corn? I LOVE Ariane, Lisa, and Myrna too, don't you? I hope it's OK I invited them to Flirt Club during rehearsal yesterday. I know—I broke all three rules! (Don't talk about Flirt Club, Don't talk about Flirt Club, Don't talk about Flirt Club.) But they were so excited, and they won't tell anyone, I don't think. I love how Myrna looks all tomboy tough but is such a girly-girl at heart. She started *squealing* when I told her about Flirt Club. And Ariane started going, "Going on a Squeegee Hunt, gonna catch a Big One." 'Member that song from, like, preschool? She's as silly as we are. Possibly sillier (is that possible?).

Well, after my big breakthrough with Sean the other day, absolutely nothing has happened. We haven't talked during class or even smiled at each other. What does a girl have to do? Isn't public humiliation enough? Isn't the hurling of paper enough? Ugh, I wish Sean was in the play. Isn't Michael Maddix a dreamy Joseph? Mmmm, he's a tasty little morsel indeed. Lucky-duck Shelly Scott.

So, Flirt Club Saturday?

I won't see you at your locker after school 'cause I'm going over to Ariane's to study for a Spanish test. Bleck (to the test, not to Ariane) AND, far more importantly, she's going to show me what hair products she uses to make her lovely raven curls so shiny and compliant (versus my sproingy bad-boys).

Love,
Bean (there done that)

Bean,

Yes, we're definitely on for Flirt Club—Saturday is good. THOSE GIRLS BETTER NOT TELL ANYONE OR I WILL DIE. DON'T TELL PEOPLE WITHOUT CONSULTING WITH ME. After all, it is a matter of national security. We can meet at my house, if you want. We can come up with a plan of attack/mission for the Sean situation at the meeting, yes? (If you're comfortable talking about it in front of the other girls/cornstalks). I bet they'll have some ideas. OK, can't write long, have test.

Love,
Cisco

🌀 🌀 🌀

Izzy (Cisco)'s Journal

Actually, I'm kind of miffed that Annie told those other girls about Flirt Club. I mean they're really nice, and they didn't think it was dorky and they got excited when she asked them, but IT WAS OUR SECRET. What if they'd thought we were total dorks? Or what if they let it slip out by accident? In some ways Annie and I are really different. I mean, I think if anyone else found out about Flirt Club, Annie might enjoy the attention and drama, whereas I would just die of embarrassment. I think I'm a more private person.

Oh well, it's probably not such a big deal. I *do* wish she'd asked me first before inviting them. It will probably end up being tons of fun. I'm just a little shy around those girls still. Annie says she's shy, but she's not as shy as I am. I feel nervous about having those girls over this weekend. I'll have to make sure the house isn't too messy. And I'm also nervous about the

Halloween dance 'cause I bet anything that Enrique will ask me to dance, and unless I'm rude and say no, that will be super weird 'cause Annie doesn't know about how much attention he pays me. I don't know what to do. Also, I really AM starting to get a crush on Michael again. FLUP. It's useless having a crush on him. But I find myself spending time in rehearsals waiting to see if he looks at me, or miracle of all miracles, smiles! But even though that happens sometimes, IT ABSOLUTELY CAN'T MEAN ANYTHING 'cause he's going out with Shelly Scott, only, like, the most popular girl in 8th grade.

Ugh. OK, I won't think about him. I just won't.

Michael Maddix Michael Maddix Michael Maddix Michael Maddix Michael Maddix Michael Maddix Michael Maddix Michael Maddix Michael Maddix Michael Maddix.

OK, now I've got him out of my system.

Yep. Gone.

~~~~~~~~~~~~~~~~~~~~~~~~~~~~~~~~~~~~~~

Flirt Club Meeting #3

Present: Scribe and Secretary Annie, Founding Member Izzy, NEW MEMBERS!!—Ariane , Lisa, and Myrna.

Rules of Flirt Club:

Number one rule of Flirt Club: Never, EVER talk about Flirt Club.

Number two rule of Flirt Club: Never, EVER talk about Flirt Club

Number three rule of Flirt Club: Never, EVER tell a soul about Flirt Club.

Minutes: Our first order of business was to review the flirting techniques we'd come up with in past meetings for new members. Myrna said she'd be willing to type up a list of past and future flirting techniques so members can study them if they like. She said she'd e-mail a copy AND print up a copy for each of us. We took a vote—All in favor of getting copies of the techniques said, "Aye-Aye, Captain!" (Everyone). Myrna's da bomb!

Then we opened the floor for new members to add any flirting techniques to our list.

New ideas:

Myrna: Bump into people you like "by accident" in the hall, classroom, or lunch line.

Myrna: Drop stuff "by accident" near a cute boy and see if he'll help you pick it up.

Ariane: If you want to get a certain boy's attention, give him a long, slow wink! I personally would be physically and emotionally unable to carry out the winking technique with a boy, but we did spend about 10 minutes practicing winking at each other—slow winks, fast winks, multiple winks that were more like facial twitches. We decided that as members of Flirt

Club, when we pass in the hall, instead of saying hi or waving we will now wink/twitch at each other.

Izzy can't wink (both her eyes close), so if she chooses to use this new technique, she will have to *blink* at Actual Designated Target.

Lisa said, quote: "I have no idea how to flirt. I've never had a boyfriend, I can hardly look at guys, much less wink at them."

THAT'S OK! We made up a new rule:

> Rule number four: There's no pressure in Flirt Club—it's for fun and you only have to do what feels right for you!

We all concurred that Lisa seems to be from a different time altogether. Izzy said it's like she stepped right out of a Rembrandt painting—very serene and shiny (not oily-skin shiny but shiny from the inside out). I suggested that perhaps Lisa's destiny is not to wink but to recline on a divan and be brought fruit by men. Or boys. Or man-boys. Izzy said *she* wanted that destiny, and Myrna said, "Me too!" So we decided that we all get to have the divan destiny if we want it (← what a bunch of kooks). Ariane said she wanted to recline on a divan, be fed chocolate, *and* wink at every passing fellow.

Then we proceeded to talk about Michael Maddix for about 15 minutes and how he's a stone fox. And then we practiced signing our names "Mrs. Maddix," "Mrs. Higgins," and

"Mrs. Alvarez" for another 10 minutes, though Lisa said she'd never give up her last name for a man, so she practiced signing "Mrs. Newcomb-Maddix" hyphenated. We all practiced hyphenated names too. I prefer plain old "Mrs. Higgins," thank you very much! Though we all agreed "Mrs. Higgins" sounds like a plump old lady who sits on her porch on a rocker and offers you fresh baked cookies as you walk home from school.

All in favor of what a stone fox Michael Maddix is said, "AYE-AYE!" (everyone).

Captain, oh my Captain!

We unanimously voted that M.M. (Michael Maddix) is the S.F. (stone fox). We unanimously decided that for our practice session, we're going to Rick's Ice Cream Parlor on Middlefield Road. We thought we might try the winking, the wallet dropping, or the "accidental" bumping technique out.

Myrna said she felt sorry for any boys who might be there because we'll all be bumping into them—they'll get all jostled around and wonder if they are at an ice cream parlor or a roller derby.

Then we made up new lyrics to the Monkee's theme song while jumping on Izzy's bed. Our version goes like this:

"Here we are, jumpin' up and down
Messin' up your covers,
but don't you frown . . .

Hey hey we're alive!
People thought we were dead
But we were only joking
We were just in bed
We just wanted to try
To see what it's like to die
We're the young generation
And we don't want you to cry."

Off to Rick's.

Report on practice session: *Not a particularly fruitful practice session*! There were only two boys at Rick's, and they were, like, about 6 years old. So we didn't bump into them or practice any flirting with them whatsoever. We *did* practice our new song and walking down the street arm in arm singing like The Monkees (with Myrna in the middle being rolled on her skateboard).

At home we DID practice the "striking up a conversation" method on each other (Ariane interspersed some heavy-duty winking in her conversation—thus her new nickname, "Twitchy").

Our assignment: Next week at rehearsal (or in class) we ALL have to implement at least ONE flirting technique from list provided by Myrna.

In Conclusion/Things we have learned at Flirt Club:

1. Asking questions is always a good start for the Flirtatiously Challenged (ALL OF US!!).
2. If we do try the new flirting technique of "accidentally bumping into" a Designated Target, we shouldn't do it all at once or the Designated Target may think we're some kind of girl gang trying to rough him up.
3. The banana ice cream at Rick's is FANTABULOSO!
4. SO IS THE MINT CHIP (says Myrna).
5. All Flirt Club assignments are highly encouraged but OPTIONAL!
6. No one knows what happened to Davy Jones from the Monkees, BUT if we could travel back in time, we'd all like to marry him.
7. Davy? Where are you Davy? Davy Joooones . . . ?
8. Myrna will type up Flirt Club list of techniques. (Myrna Rocks!)
9. Flirt Club rocks!
10. We need a replacement word for "rocks!" "Rocks" does not rock.
11. Suggestions for replacement words for "rocks":
    ☆ Crackles
    ☆ Fangles!
    ☆ Cracks! (too druggy?)

- ☆ Bangs! (too sexy?)
- ☆ Rips!
- ☆ Flares!
- ☆ Toots! (my personal favorite, though apparently a synonym for "farts"; you learn something new every day)

OK, obviously we haven't discovered a good replacement word for "rocks" yet.

Then Izzy got an old, empty photo album and we started our Flirt Club Scrapbook/Almanac. Right now the only things in it are the wrinkly note that Sean gave me that says "HI ANNIE" on it and a napkin Lisa had from Rick's that says "Rick's Ice Cream" on one side and "Flirt Club Toots!" on the other. Goshly jeezly, what a bunch of dorks! The club should be called "Dork Club," not Flirt Club!!!

For the last order of business we tried to come up with a regular time to meet (like every other Saturday), but that proved difficult (apparently we're all very busy and important people. Lisa is part of a Bollywood dance troupe *and* she helps design their costumes. How cool is that?). So we decided to meet whenever we can all make it, ideally twice a month.

And thus concludes the third meeting of Dork Club—I mean, Flirt Club.

Myrna's List

FLIRT CLUB TECHNIQUES

1. Flip hair. (This is a good technique for people with silky, longish hair.)
2. Bite the end of a pencil (not too hard though!) and look up at Designated Target with mischief in the eyes, like one knows a good secret.
3. Ask questions about ANYTHING (and I mean anything . . . like, "Why do you think they made pencils yellow?").
4. Listen to answer like it's the most fascinating thing in the world.
5. Laugh and giggle A LOT, like whatever Designated Target says is witty (use techniques 1 through 5 at your discretion—they may be a little ditsy!).
6. Smack Designated Target (again, not too hard, and usually on the back of his head or shoulder area).
7. Throw things at Designated Target (usually crumpled-up paper—FOOD, NOT SO GOOD!).
8. If a guy looks at you, try to look back instead of immediately looking away.

9. If a guy looks at you and you are able to keep looking, try to go for a smile if you think he's cute.

10. Practice being friendly and conversational with people you don't know very well, even if they aren't people you want to flirt with (including cats and old ladies).

11. If you have a question about something (a real one, not a dumb one), try to ask a cute boy.

12. Bump into Designated Target "by accident" in the hall, classroom, or lunch line.

13. Drop stuff "by accident" near a Designated Target and see if he'll help you pick it up.

14. If you want to get a Designated Target's attention, give him a wink. (Not for the faint of heart!)

6

I Could Have Danced All Night

Dear Cisco,

A miracle happened today! After English, Sean waited for me and walked with me to Center Quad, and while we were walking he asked me if I was going to the Halloween dance this Friday and I said yes. He didn't ask me to go WITH him—just if I was going—BUT STILL!!!!!! And the miracle continued to unfold as I was able to continue the conversation (A DIRECT RESULT FROM FLIRT CLUB!!) and ask him what he was going to be for Halloween. He said he was going to be John McEnroe and I stared at him blankly with big fish eyes, and he laughed and said that John McEnroe was a famous old-school tennis player. I guess Sean is a tennis fan/player?

Anyhoo, he asked me what I was going to be and I said I was going to be the Queen of the Nile! Where did I come up with that?

I pulled it right out of my butt!

Out of thin air! The truth is I hadn't contemplated what I was going to be at all, but I guess I AM going to be Queen of the Nile. He talked to me! And then he touched my shoulder and said he'd see me later.

My shoulder!

Later!

Woop dee pooo! And other celebratory sounds! Like yippy tow wow yea!

Fandango!

Write me back, my little glossy-coated pony princess! My little Hamburger Helper! What?

Can you tell I'm a little giddy?

If Sean really likes me, if something happens at the Halloween dance, then I'm gonna have to break up with Enrique's ear. Enrique's ear probably won't take it too hard since it never knew we were dating!

What are you gonna be for Halloween? Maybe all of Flirt Club (aka The Dancing Corn Alliance) could all go together??

Weeee! And other less dorky celebratory sounds!

~Bean Bean the hyper fruit

P.S. I made you this collage during my free period, view it and weep: it represents us and our experience of school dances to date. But we're much cooler now, right? Please tell me I'm right.

Bean,

That rocks! I mean, it toots! Or it flarps! Yes, I think we're cooler, I think we toot! (And so, I disprove my point.) Really, that's great about Sean. It seems like he likes you. You probably said Queen of the Nile 'cause Margaret Pope was measuring us for our Egyptian costumes yesterday for *Joseph*? Too bad we can't use our *Joseph* costumes at the dance. Oh well. What should I be? Here are some ideas:

> Princess Leia (NOT Princess Leia in the gold
> bikini chained to Jabba the Hut)
> A mermaid (aka a mer-blob)
> Mrs. Dracula
> Hip-Hop Rapunzel (though don't know how
> I'd portray that)????

Remember when we were Melanie and Scarlet from *Gone with the Wind*? And we pretended that Emmet (poor child) was Ashley and we fought over him all night in Southern accents as we tromped from house to house? That was so fun! But we probably scarred him for life, psychologically speaking. And my mom made us those skirts with hula hoops in them? That totally tooted!

Hey! Maybe you could be the Queen of the Nile and I could BE the Nile! Like, I could dress all in watery colors and flowing garments. Or maybe I could be your slave boy and fan you all night! That sounds tiring though. We'll see . . .

Maybe I'll do something wildly out of character and ask Michael Maddix to dance.

NOT! We both know I couldn't do that even if my life depended on it. Maybe I could do it if YOUR life depended on it, though.

M.M. is the S.F.

Sigh . . . and other sounds that represent dorky longing.

OK, Mrs. Higgins, have to go now.

Love,
Mrs. Maddix

P.S. Destroy this note immediately, Agent 66, with your high-powered government-sanctioned laser document incinerator!!!!!!!!!!!!!

Cisco,

Well, tonight's the night! And so far my Queen of the Nile costume kind of sucks! I'm wearing this old 60s gold lamé housecoat of my mom's, tied with this blue scarf/sash thing and this gold-and-blue stripy scarf-thing of Ariane's for an Egyptian headdress. LOTS O' EYE MAKEUP is the key!

Myrna's rope sandals will be perfect. I tried the whole thing on for Ariane and she said it was sexy, and frankly, at this point I'll take sexy over historically accurate!! *Hello!*

Lisa's costume is super sexy; she's wearing her Bollywood dance outfit. Have you seen it? Can you get kicked out of a dance for revealing your midriff? I hope not.

You definitely made the right choice being Princess Leia. It's FINE that your costume is an old white choir robe of your mother's, it TOTALLY makes you look like Princess Leia when she's all "Obi Wan, you're my only hope." Just tie something around the waist and do the two big doughnuts for hair—that'll look awesome. You definitely have the hair for it!

Let's put my glitter lotion on OK? It's good for both of us 'cause I'm a gilded Egyptian queen and you're supposed to be sci-fi. Boys love Princess Leia! Your dance card will be quite full, madam!

Love,
Bean

P.S. I'm so excited and I just can't hide it!
P.P.S. "Sean Higgins, you're my only hope."

Dear My Only Hope (aka Bean),
Oh, I wish we had dance cards! I wish, I wish! Instead of standing around hoping someone will ask us to dance. Things

were so much more civilized back in the *Pride and Prejudice* days! The dances were so *structured,* each person knew exactly what to do and when. There was none of this random wiggling your body around right in front of a boy in hopes of appearing rhythmic and attractive (perhaps even, God forbid, sexy!). Geez laweez, the pressure! I can't take it, I'm going to explode! Nah, not really.

I guess *we're* free to ask boys to dance too, but that's for normal girls who aren't so shy that they want to hide their head in one of those gaps in the bleachers. Do you think I could *fit* my head in one of those gaps? If this dance is as embarrassing as our Spring Fling last year, I may just have to try it (sticking my head in the gap).

Hey, Bean, do you still have my striped stockings? I told Myrna she could borrow them for her and Ariane's rag-doll costumes. Myrna's gonna make up her mouth and eyes to look like they're stitched closed, like a zombie rag doll, MWA-HA-Haaaaa. I heard that Cathy Greenwood and the girls in the popular group are going as jocks, and the jocks/popular boys are going as cheerleaders. So I wonder what M.M. will be. He's in that group but he's not a jock exactly. I wonder if he'll be a cheerleader.

Well, I'll find out tonight.

Love,
Cisco

◎ ◎ ◎

Izzy's Journal

I'm home from the Halloween dance and I don't even know where to start, it was such a weird night!! Well, first of all, one weird thing was that Enrique showed up as Luke Skywalker! So people kept going, "Hey, Leia, there's Luke," about a million times! Pretty embarrassing. I just kept trying to ignore them, laugh it off, etc., and I could tell it kind of bothered Annie. Ugh. And shortly after we got there, we were standing by the stage with the Cornstalk Alliance, aka Flirt Club, and Nick Cassalas and Enrique come and stand right near us. Enrique kept smiling at me and I kept trying not to look at him 'cause Annie's right there, BUT also I didn't want to hurt his feelings/be rude. A BASICALLY IMPOSSIBLE SITUATION! So we girls start practicing our "Monkees Theme" dance and Enrique walks right up 'cause I'm on the end and goes, "Madam may I have this dance?" (almost like he knows my Jane Austen fixation). And I *couldn't* say no, it just felt too mean. So I go out onto the dance floor and catch a glimpse of Annie's face, which is shocked and turning red. Lord, I wanted to hide in a crack in the floor, I felt so bad. So, Enrique's doing all these swing dance moves, whirling me around and stuff (which would have been SO fun if I wasn't worried about Annie), and one of my Princess Leia buns flies loose and my undone hair starts whipping him in the head! Then he pretended he was under attack from a giant squid tentacle (my hair) while we were dancing, and I couldn't help it, I started to laugh and laugh and have WAY too much fun.

After the dance was over, he just stands in front of me, smiling and holding on to my wrists, and I go, all awkward-like, "Thanks," and basically run away. When I get back to the girls, Annie raises her eyebrows at me like "What was that?" and I just shrug. She didn't seem mad, just kind of quiet. And I felt weird even though we were all goofing off and practicing our corn dance to that "ooga-chaka ooga-chaka" song that was playing on the loudspeaker. THEN Sean Higgins (who we'd been looking for and couldn't find) came over and pulled Annie out onto the dance floor! He didn't even ask her to dance—just pulled her away! I was totally happy for Annie and relieved, but Lisa said he smelled like beer.

Anyhow, Sean and Annie danced like FIVE dances in a row, including a slow one! During the slow dance, Enrique started coming toward me and I darted away—silly, silly rabbit! I actually *really* wanted to slow dance with him. I should have talked to Annie about him a long time ago. I just didn't know what to say. (AND STILL DON'T.)

During the rest of the dance I danced a few more times— a couple of times with some 7th-grade boys whom I don't even know, once with Danny Rosenberg (!), and then one more time with Enrique when he successfully snuck up on me and I didn't have a chance to dart away. It was a slow dance! Annie was busy dancing with Sean again (they danced together on and off for most of the night) and I didn't feel like I could say no to him. Plus I WANTED TO DANCE WITH HIM! Someone from yearbook took a picture of us 'cause we were Luke and Leia dancing together, and I guess they thought it was romantic. It was romantic . . . for me at least!

Near the end of the evening, a couple of weird things happened. Madison Geller asked Sean Higgins to dance two times in a row, and then Mia Shepard asked him to dance, and Annie and I basically just stood by the bleachers and tried to act like we didn't mind being on the sidelines. Annie was acting all chipper and stuff, but her face looked a little forlorn and worried. Why did those popular girls have to hone in on Sean? I mean, they can have any boy in the school.

ANYWAY, weirdest of all weirdnesses, I CAN'T BELIEVE who asked me to dance for the next-to-last dance: Michael Maddix!!! I still can't believe it. I mean, he danced with Shelly for most of the night and some of those other popular girls, BUT THEN HE ASKED ME. AND WE HAD FUN. It was like we were back in fourth grade again and just playing around like we used to before everything got all weird as far as people getting into different cliques. We danced like Egyptians 'cause of the Egyptian dance in *Joseph,* and we tried to sing *Joseph* lyrics: "Way, way back many centuries ago" to the rock song that was playing. IT WAS REALLY FUN. I AM IN SHOCK. Is he a drama geek at heart?

I like two people right now, Michael Maddix and Enrique (yes, I have to admit I like him even though Annie does/did too), and I got to dance with both of those guys tonight!

It's a miracle! Maybe Flirt Club and the play ARE helping me be less shy. Thank the god of singing cornstalks. Thank the tiny gods of glitter lotion. I have to sleep now.

@ @ @

Dear Cisco,

I just had a VERY interesting conversation with Enrique in Center Quad. He was asking me about you, if you had a boyfriend and stuff. I said no. I think he likes you! You really should go out with him if you like him. My affair with his ear has cooled down a lot since Sean came into the picture. I mean maybe it was fate that you dressed like Princess Leia and he dressed like Luke Skywalker. Who am I to stand in the way of Destiny with a capital "D"?

I can tell you this: he's really nice and his ear is a magical miniature wonderland.

Those are my recommendations.

So, I am so nervous to see Sean. I haven't seen him all day and we'll see each other in English next period. I mean he was almost acting like my boyfriend at the dance. I'm just a tiny bit worried he likes Madison or Mia now. Oh, my palms are sweating. Anyhoo, whatever happens, we're certainly making progress aren't we, Agent #88? Our mission to explore strange new boys, to boldly flirt where no one has flirted before (except, of course, Jeannie Mateo) is going quite well.

I bet if Michael Maddix wasn't going out with Shelly Scott he'd ask you out!!!

M.M. is the S.F.!!!!!

Ooooo, I have butterflies in my stomach, the bell rang. Time to see Sean.

Time to face the music

Time to bite the bullet

Time to bite the music

Time to face the musical bullet while biting a bull. (That's what it feels like!!!)

I'll write a full report and have it on your desk (aka, the bottom of your locker) by 7th period.

Love,
Bean

Addendum!!! It is now later on!! I can write 'cause Enrique and I finished our lab. So, the news is not great, not great at all. Here's what happened: I'm sitting in English (Sean's not there yet) and I'm staring at the door like a small dog waiting and shivering for a doggy treat. So he comes in, walks to his desk, sits down, and doesn't look at me right away. But then he turns around and gives me a friendly-ish smile (I think I sense a coolness in the smile though). I grimace back at him in a twitchy, convulsive way (OH YEAH, I'M A CHARMER, ALL RIGHT!) and he just turns around and opens his book and doesn't try to talk to me or throw anything or *anything* even though Mrs. Kelly wasn't even there yet! We have absolutely no interactions for the rest of the class. Except for me staring fretfully at the shiny hair on the back of his head. And then it was time to leave and he kind of HURRIED out the door without looking at me once. It was almost like he was avoiding me. No more smiles or conversation. Oh, this doesn't bode well. Not boding well. Bad, bad boding.

"Bode" is such a weird word. Say it a bunch of times in your head . . . see what I mean?

Well, crap on a stick. Sean and I danced 11 dances! YES, I COUNTED. YES, I'm A DORK. Doesn't that mean anything??

Oh Cisco, I'm deflated like the red balloon in that French movie they made us watch every year in elementary school. Remember? How the little boy chases it, going, *"Ballon, ballon,"* in French and something else happens that I can't remember, and then the balloon sits too long in the sun and they have this time-lapse thing where it gets a little more shriveled in every shot till it's a little old dead red prune balloon? And the little boy is so sad and then all the balloons from all over the city start traveling toward him at hyper-speed and they arrive and he grabs them all and he flies away or some such happy business.

"Ballon, ballon . . ." (said with a melancholy French accent).
Is Sean my shriveling red balloon?

Is our love over before it began?

If I wasn't truly unhappy, would I be enjoying this opportunity to be deliciously maudlin? Oh, Cisco . . . so many questions on this sad day of reckoning and shriveling dreams.

Not to mention wrinkled red balloons.

Write me back.

Can you come over after school?

In love and some woe,
~Bean

Bean,

Well, bummer about Sean . . . BUT DO NOT GIVE UP HOPE ENTIRELY!! Maybe he was just feeling shy or "taking some space" as my sister's boyfriend is so fond of doing. Though my sister says that "taking space" is actually code for being a big chicken butt with "serious intimacy issues." Um . . . whatever. Of course I can come over, we only have rehearsal on Wednesday and Thursday this week, sí? Correct, my little tortilla?

I can't believe those popular girls started in on Sean at the dance. I mean, aren't all the totally cute boys in their own group enough for them?

I say don't give up on Sean yet; we don't know for sure what's happening with him. You are the bestest, most adorable girl, and Sean is a social-climbing turd if he'd choose one of those girls over you.

Yes, I'm coming over after school.

In love and frustration
(for your sake),
Cisco

P.S. Thanks for telling me that stuff about Enrique. He IS cute. I don't know about dating him or anything, we'll see. And besides M.M. is the S.F. and my future husband.

7

Thwarted in the Season of Love

Cisco,

Bad news. Besides the fact that Sean and I didn't really talk or anything *all* last week, Myrna said she heard from Beth Stark that Sean went to Madison Geller's party this weekend, AND I saw them sitting together at the end of lunch period today. Just the two of them. I knew it! I knew he was acting weird and ignoring me. I mean, I thought it may have been my imagination, but it seemed like he felt *guilty* in English class. I don't know, it's not like he did anything obvious, it just sort of wafted out of the back of his shiny head. Like Jeannie Mateo's stinky perfume. Flup. Madison is totally cute and popular, so who can blame him? Now he'll probably be part of that group. I'm bummed. I've been thwarted (love that word). Thwarted in the season of love.

Here's a poem called "Thwarted in the Season of Love":
(By an anonymous author who is feeling very thwarted)

Thwarted in the Season of Love
I!
Am Thwarted!
Can you tell how thwarted I am
By my limp dangling arms
And droopy-eyed demeanor?
If you can't
Well . . . know this—
I!
Am Thwarted!
Thwarted in the Season of Love!

OK, I know it's a flupping poo-poo poem—you're the poet—but I need art therapy.

Oh Cisco, time to pull myself up by the bootstraps again.

Flup, my bootstraps are getting pretty stretched out, pretty long in the tooth.

Gotta go. Let's convene Flirt Club this weekend; I need something to look forward to.

Love,
Bean

P.S. I swear to Gump that Michael Maddix would like you if it weren't for Shelly. Did you notice when he's on stage and we're watching he seems like he's performing for you? He's always goofing & trying to catch your eye and always looking over to see if you're watching!!

M.M. is the S.F.

Dear Bean,

Well, poo on Sean. Actually, Sean IS poo. So poo on him, the big ol' social climbing piece of poo. Poo on top of poo. Double stinky trouble. I'm sorry, Beanster. Here's my analysis: Sean liked you. You liked him. Then some of the popular (or should I say *poop*ular) girls noticed that Sean was a Tasty Little Nugget and decided to see if they could turn his tasty little head. And they did. So, the final conclusion must be that Sean is not the one for you. The One For You would not be so easily wooed by another, you know?

To reiterate: Sean is a big piece of poo climbing up a social ladder. (Visualize that.)

Yes, yes, yes, Flirt Club this weekend. I'll tell Lisa, and you tell Myrna and Ariane.

Love,
Cisco

P.S. Michael Maddix is always looking at ALL of the girls in the chorus to see if we're watching—he loves the attention.

I don't think it's directed at me in particular. Though I certainly wouldn't mind if it was!! Because . . .

M.M. is the S.F.

~~~~~~

Izzy's Diary

I can't believe Sean pulled a switch-a-roo on Annie. I'm pretty sure he's going steady with Madison now. I saw them walking together after school holding hands. Ugh. Why did he pay so much attention to Annie and then TOTALLY IGNORE HER? Poor Annie-Bean. I also wish he still liked her for selfish reasons—then I wouldn't feel guilty about Enrique. I like him a little bit more all the time. He likes to pull my hair (gently) in English and make some sort of sound effects. Like a car horn or doorbell or animal noises. Today he pulled it and made the sound of a flushing toilet and said in an English accent, "Hmm, splendid plumbing they've installed in this place!" He makes me laugh. And I like it when he touches my hair. I get tingles that go up my spine to my head. He's pretty cute. I just feel like it would be uncaring to go out with him when Annie's sad about Sean AND she used to like Enrique. The timing is all off. She says it won't bother her if he and I go out . . . But!!! Not too long ago she spent an entire day composing a flower card for him! I don't really know what to do. Plus, who I like even more is Michael Maddix. It's useless fighting the old crush. He

DOES pay special attention to me during rehearsal—Annie's right. Boy, he is SO dreamy when he sings! He's really charismatic on stage. I'm SO glad I tried out for *Joseph*—I've never had so much fun. I'm getting much more comfortable being around boys. There's nobody in the cast that I LIKE-like except M.M., but the guys are nice and I can talk to them a little bit. Which is better than before . . .'CAUSE BEFORE I WAS SILENT!! Off to bed.

~~~~~~

Annie-Bean's Journal

The only one for me is Nelson. Why bother with boys? Cats are better. Nelson loves me. He doesn't dance with me all night and then act like I don't exist and go live with the people next door. I'm kind of mad at Sean. I mean, I understand him choosing Madison and all, she's pretty and now he's sort of automatically included in the popular group. I love my friends and hanging out with the drama people, but I have to admit (AND I HOPE NO ONE EVER READS THIS . . . EVER!!!!), I wish I were more popular. It would be so fun to be in that group and have the whole school know who you are and have boys chasing you, etc. I wish I could go to one of their parties. I wonder what it's like. I wonder if *I'd* been the popular one and Madison was a drama geek if Sean would have chosen me instead. I'm bummed. I really thought something would happen with Sean. I've never even kissed a boy. Izzy kissed Grant

Carson in seventh grade when she played spin the bottle at Beth Stark's house and she said it was just blah. Worse than blah. Like putting your mouth on a damp fish. But she didn't even like him or anything, so I bet that changes the old fish feeling! I really wanted to kiss Sean. I kind of miss him, it's strange. I mean we hardly even spoke. I guess I miss the excitement of thinking that maybe something would happen. That maybe I'd finally get to have a real kiss. And now Enrique likes IZZY! Not that he shouldn't, she's the best; it's just a lot of disappointment. My stomach feels like it's full of tar. I wonder if I'm getting sick or if it's just plain old sadness. I'm going to make a collage to put in Izzy's locker.

Dear Bean,

School and rehearsal are so dull without you! I ate lunch with Myrna and them—thank goodness I had SOMEONE to sit with. Lisa taught us some Bollywood dance moves, which was cool. I wish I could call you, but my Mom says it's too late. She's probably right, so I'm gonna write instead and put it in your locker first thing. I hope, hope you're back tomorrow!

OK, a terrible thing happened at rehearsal and if I don't tell someone I'm going to burst. So, Michael was singing "Close Every Door" and we girls were all sitting in the audience, gazing at him with dewy eyes. I was trying to see if you were right and see if he DID look at me while he was on stage. And, well,

I seemed to notice him looking my way off and on! Which was great UNTIL (and this is ONE BIG UNTIL) he was looking right at me and I laughed at something Myrna said and you know how sometimes when you laugh with a stuffy nose (and mine is SUPER stuffy) something gross comes out? That happened.

A lot of it happened.

ALL OVER MY FACE WHILE MICHAEL MADDIX WAS LOOKING DIRECTLY AT ME. His eyebrows went up in shock, and I covered my face and ran out of the theater. AND I DIDN'T COME BACK. I got my stuff from the dressing room and just left. I missed the Egyptian scene entirely. I'll tell Mrs. P. that I felt sick and had to rush home. But, oh Annie, I'll never be able to look at M.M. again. Ever. That was the most embarrassing moment of my life. And it happened to be a private little moment shared between me and the boy of my dreams.

Life is cruel. Snot is crueler.

I am still blushing when I write this to you. Even though it is late at night and I am alone with this paper. I hope hope hope you come to school and tech rehearsal tomorrow because I can't face it (HIM) alone.

I hope you are feeling better.

Love,
Cisco

Cisco,

Oh Lordy, I just read your note! Flup! Oh dear, you poor thing. Maybe he didn't see you? Or what came out of your nose? What row were you sitting in? Were the house lights on?

Well, I'll definitely be back at rehearsal today (even though I can't sing full force) and I'll stick by your side. I'm sure even if he did see your nose explode, he won't judge you for it—boys like gross stuff, right? Did you get the collage I made you? I think if Sean tries to be buddies with me now that he's got himself a popular girlfriend (I saw him and Madison holding hands before 1st period—it's official!), I'll give him the cold shoulder. I don't think what he did was very nice. I mean, everybody has the right to change their mind, but he asked me to dance 11 TIMES. TWO SLOW DANCES. AND THOSE WERE SOME PRETTY FRIENDLY SLOW DANCES. He had me squeezed pretty flupping tight AND he was nuzzling my neck and all AND he kissed me on the cheek once. What did your sister say about players? We need to talk about players at Flirt Club, like how to identify them. Ways to know if boys are just toying with you. I have to write about something else 'cause my eyes are getting hot and wet and I can't cry in Center Quad. You know what will make me feel better? SINGING AND DANCING DRESSED UP LIKE A PIECE OF CORN!! 'Member how bummed I was when they posted that we were corn? Now I love it.

This weekend Ariane said we could have Flirt Club at her

house, and she lives right near Mayfield Mall, so we can go there to practice.

Don't worry about facing M.M. I'll be "By Your Side" . . . 'Member when we sang that duet in the 6th-grade talent show? Anyway, little does M.M. know that we're top-secret agents and that when snot appears to explode out of your nose it's in actuality an antibacterium solution that spontaneously erupts and kills invading lethal airborne viruses that only we can detect. So, what *seems* like a socially awkward moment is actually you saving the world with your nose (all in a day's work, right Agent #88?)

M.M. is the S.F.

S.H. is the B.P. (Big Poo)

~Bean

〜〜〜〜〜〜〜〜〜〜〜〜〜〜〜〜〜〜〜〜

Izzy (Cisco)'s Journal

Well, I survived going back to rehearsal. Michael Maddix didn't shun me or anything. I don't know if he ever looked into my eyes during the Egyptian scene or while we corn and the farm animals were rehearsing because I never looked him directly in the face! But he was his usual friendly self. That's good.

I can tell Enrique is confused by me. I always respond to his flirting but just barely. In English we were talking about that fountain in the middle of the mall and joking about how we should scoop out all the pennies and buy as many Swedish fish as we could with them from the candy kiosk. But then he goes, "We should do that sometime, or at least go buy some Swedish fish and put them in the fountain and see if they swim." Which, of course, made me laugh, but then it seemed like he wanted a real answer, so I go, "Yeah . . . *maybe* . . . we could do that sometiiiime . . ." or some other mealy-mouthed response, and then I start reading my own homework furiously. Oh brother. It would be cruel to Annie if anything were to happen with him right now. She's still recovering from the Sean debacle. He totally sits with Madison and them at lunch now; I bet even if he and Madison break up, he'll be part of that popular group from here on out. Sometimes I wish I was in that group, mostly because then I might have more of a chance with Michael M.

M.M. is the S.F.

I can't wait until the cast party of *Joseph*. Is it weird that I'm looking forward to the party more than the shows themselves? Oh well, I think I like singing, dancing, and rehearsing more than the actual performing. I get too much stage fright! Plus, M.M. will be at the cast party but Shelly Scott and all those popular girls can't come! Not like anything would actually happen with Michael and I. As if!!!!

Can't wait for Flirt Club this weekend!

<u>Flirt Club Minutes (Official Meeting #4)</u>

(Scribe Annie) Fantabulous other members present: Izzy, Ariane, and Myrna (Lisa had to rehearse with her Bollywood troupe)

May the meeting of the singing, dancing corn commence!

First off, we admired the blue streaks Myrna put in her blond hair. She said what she really wanted was to get an onyx tattoo on her ankle, but her parents said, "N.O. NO."

Topic number one: ***How to recognize a player***.

As Izzy so aptly said, "What *is* a player anyway?"
Our limited thoughts on the matter:

1. A player is someone who flirts with you to get you to like them but who may not actually like you or want to go out with you.

2. A player is someone who acts like they like you more than they do to try to "score" (sexually).

3. A player is someone who likes to collect women like a cowboy likes to collect decorative belt buckles (according to Myrna).

Signs that you may be dealing with a player:

☆ His eyes dart around, looking at other girls when he talks to you.

☆ He doesn't follow through with what he says he'll do.

☆ He may be super effusive or complimentary but not kind in his actions.

☆ Basically we're just flying by the seat of our pants here; we're all abysmally inexperienced.

~~~~~~

Reports of flirting activity commenced since our last meeting:

Myrna: Myrna reported that she tried the dropping-something technique twice. Once she dropped her science book at Chris Jordasch's feet (his locker is next to hers) and said, "Oh drat!" (which she regrets, feeling "Drat" is an outdated exclamation). Chris looked at the book, looked at her, hoisted his backpack on, slammed his locker closed, and walked away.

Chivalry is DEAD! (Flirt Club takes a moment of silence to mourn chivalry.)

She also dropped her pencil during math because the Stone Fox himself sits next to her. Mr. Poff happened to be walking down her aisle and picked it up saying, "Here you go, young lady, it looks like your pencil is trying to run away!"

Chivalry is not dead! At least when it comes to nerdy, middle-aged math teachers!

Ariane: Ariane had a very successful time starting up conversations with boys. She started up numerous conversations with boys—though none of the boys were particularly attractive to her. She said it was easier to start by talking to boys that "didn't give her that special feeling"—taking baby steps as it were.

We gave three hearty cheers to Ariane's baby steps. Though Ariane said there may be drawbacks to this technique because both Glenn Gould and Brian Ellis have begun trotting down the halls to catch up with her when they see her. They may be smitten. Hmmmmm. Are WE turning into players? This is so confusing!!! Why isn't there a guidebook?

Ariane's thoughts: "I don't think just talking to a boy whom you're not interested in romantically makes you a player. But maybe flirting with him does?"

We have nothing but shrugs. We are inexperience wrapped in dorkdom.

Jeannie Mateo flirts all the time, is she a player? Why are girls who flirt called "a tease" and boys who flirt called "charming" or "a player"? Why does the girls' label presume that she owes something more than flirting and the boys' label implicate sports? Why isn't there a class about THIS stuff at school? My cannoli head is stuffed with questions!!!!

We gave three cheers to the fact that we all ended up dancing with boys at the Halloween dance versus hiding our heads in the bleachers (even though the particular fate that befell me after the dance was one of great suckage and woe). I told everyone how my life is like the little red balloon movie, especially when the red balloon shrivels in the sun. Myrna patted my hair and Ariane put sparkle-flower appliqués on my fingernails. We didn't get around to a practice session because

a) We got temporarily distracted/inspired and choreographed a dance skit to "I Don't Know How to Love Him" from *Jesus Christ Superstar*! Myrna plays Jesus and the rest of us play three Mary Magdalenes tortured by longing—taking turns alternately lip-syncing, posing, and writhing around on the ground while Jesus reads the paper distractedly while rolling cross-legged on a skateboard (it devolves into a scooting battle to have Jesus for ourselves, cleaving him unto our tortured bosom). We talked about doing it for the school talent show. They'd throw tomatoes for sure.

b) We went to Mayfield Mall but we spent all our time at the Earring Hut and the Limited and how many boys are you gonna see at the Earring Hut? Zero! But Myrna bought the cutest hoodie. Then, before we left, we took turns riding Myrna's skateboard around this empty parking lot. SUPER fun!

c) My mom wanted me to pick up ingredients for stuffing (I'm making it this year!), so the girls accompanied me to the grocery store and

whipped me with celery stalks and such. I love
my girls.

Our between-meeting assignment: to keep studying the list
that Myrna so beautifully compiled and practice the techniques outlined therein!

And thus adjourns the fourth official meeting of Flirt
Club.

P.S. We didn't have anything to add to our Flirt Club
Scrapbook that Izzy lugged all the way over. Oh well.

8

What Does It Mean If He Has a Girlfriend but Stuffs Other Girls into Closets?

Dear Cisco,

I can't believe *Joseph* is almost over. It went by in such a whir! I'm not a bad person am I? I feel so bad that I started laughing when Christopher Ray slipped last night during the opening scene. It's just that a singing, dancing, chubby sheep falling on its butt is so funny! *He* was laughing too! Luckily I'm not in the front row so probably no one in the audience could see me. But geez, I actually have sore stomach muscles from laughing so hard. And then me and my Egyptian wig! Flying off during Potiphar's song. OMG, your and Myrna's shoulders were SHAKING, you were laughing so hard. She told me later that some drool came out of her mouth during the whole wig fiasco. OH CISCO! I don't want the show to be over. What if I cry at the cast party? What if I'm the biggest drama queen in the history of all drama geeks throughout history?

I have to buy lunch today, but I'll see you at the usual spot?

Love,
Bean

Dear Bean,

It was funny enough when your wig *flew* off, but then Myrna kept stepping on it and kicking it around with her feet as she danced, and *then* she just *punts* it over to you like we were a soccer team. I laughed so hard while we were changing into our rainbow costumes that tears were streaming down my face. And Margaret kept going, "Are you all right? Are you all right?" and then she started laughing too even though she had no idea what we were laughing about because we couldn't speak to tell her!

OK, I'll see you at our usual spot.

Love,
Cisco

@ @ @

Izzy's Journal

Tomorrow is the last performance of *Joseph* and the cast party. Since it's a Sunday, we have a matinee, a break, our final evening show, and then THE PARTY!! I'm simultaneously TOTALLY EXCITED for the party and TOTALLY BUMMED IT'S OVER! By now I'm almost positive that Michael Maddix *does* pay extra attention to me. Annie's right. It's not just wishful thinking. When I was leaving the girls' dressing room after last night's show, he was standing there, leaning against the wall chewing on a straw and he walks out with me like he'd been waiting for me. He asked me if I was going to the cast party. I said, "Of course," and he goes, "Are you bringing anyone, a boyfriend or something?" And HERE'S THE THING—HE SEEMED NERVOUS!!! And I go, "No," and I can feel myself turning 100 shades of red, and I giggle like a moron and then we stop 'cause we're at the exit, and he goes, "So, there isn't anyone special?" And I totally lost my ability to speak, and I was just staring at my left sneaker. I literally could not talk. And he's all, "No one you particularly like?" and I made a kind of strangled noise (NOT AN ACTUAL WORD OF ANY KIND!) and looked up in his eyes. And that look said it all. I couldn't hide that HE was my someone special. And I had to bolt and go over to where the girls were. I couldn't even say good-bye.

And he just walked away, singing at the top of his lungs,

"MAY MEE MY MOE MOO, MAY MEE MY MOE MOO!" the vocal warm-ups Mr. Libratore makes us do before every show!

The girls and I went to Denny's afterward and we discussed the whole thing. Though I felt a little strange being all excited because I know Annie still feels a little bummed over Sean. AND none of us really know for sure but we think Michael is still with Shelly Scott.

SO WHAT'S HAPPENING?

We decided that the likelihood of Michael Maddix being a player was about 74% to 26% in favor of playerhood. But then why can't I stop liking him?

We all discussed how if he "put the moves on us," girlfriend or no, we *may* not be able to resist, he's such a charmer. Well, except Lisa. Lisa Proud and Tall. I don't want to have any romantic involvement with a guy who has a girlfriend, but I've only loved M.M. since first grade. I mean, jeez, he used to come over to my house. I remember one time when he was over playing with me and Dawn and these older girls were coming over for a playdate and we were embarrassed to be playing with a boy. So we dressed Michael in one of Dawn's dresses and put a headband on his tawny locks! He looked like a totally cute (if a little rugged) girl! We told the older girls his name was Mary and he kept skipping around the yard singing, "Skip to my loo, skip to my loo, my darling!" in this high, squeaky voice. The girls thought (s)he was weird, but I don't think they ever caught on. We called him Mary for a year but he never minded. I wonder if he remembers all this.

Anyway, I CAN'T WAIT FOR THE CAST PARTY!! I have no idea what is up with Mr. Maddix, but I do know we girls will have fun NO MATTER WHAT! It's gonna be at Mrs. P.'s house. She's so cool.

@ @ @

Dear Big Booty Number 3 (I love that game) aka Cisco,

OK! What happened with you and M.M. last night after I left the cast party?? (Stupid, stupid curfew!!!!) Because OMG, Myrna keeps trying to mumble something about a slow dance? But Mrs. Heinick is watching us like a hawk. We can't even whisper in this class. Write me a note as soon as you get this— I'm going to run like the wind after math to get this in your locker before second period. Last night was so fun. I LOVED playing Big Booty and Sardines and when we did "I Don't Know How to Love Him" with our Jesus on a skateboard, people laughed! I love drama geeks. I can't believe *Joseph* is over. I wonder what the next show is going to be. Promise me you'll be in it!

Write me right away. I can't wait until lunch to get an update.

Love,
Bear

Dear Bean,

Promise me you'll feed this note to a llama as soon as you read it. PROMISE. I know we always say that, but this time I mean it. Thank God I have my free period so I am free to tell you EVERYTHING—unbosom myself as it were. YES, there was a slow dance. OK, OK, I'll start from when you left. Well, after you left, we were all dancing to ABBA for a while—I love ABBA—and then Michael goes over and starts flipping through the CDs and puts on this slow song, "Moving Pictures, Silent Films," by the Great Lake Swimmers. Do you know it? I looooove it. Then he beelines over to me and asks me to dance. And I said yes (OF COURSE! ARE YOUR EYES POPPING OUT OF YOUR HEAD YET?). So we're slow dancing in the living room and most everybody else groans and clears out (except Katie Chethik and Wes Lee, who are practically married), so we're almost alone in Mrs. P.'s living room *slow dancing.* And, of course I was dying and pretty much melting on the spot but also feeling a little weird 'cause what about Shelly Scott? Are they still together? So it's just us four in the living room, and Wes and Michael are, like, making faces or gesturing at each other or something—I couldn't see their faces, right, 'cause my face is sort of snuggled in Michael's shoulder. And finally Michael groans, *"Man"* at Wes and PICKS ME UP and carries me into the coat closet and closes the door BEHIND US! I kid you not. WE'RE ALONE IN THE CLOSET. It's totally dark and squishy 'cause of all the coats. And I panic. I feel his face sort of brush my cheek and I think he's going to kiss me and I feel like I'm gonna pass out, so I go, "Umm, I can't breathe," and grope for the doorknob and let myself out. He just goes, "Well, be that way," and laughs and closes the door **with him still in the closet** and me outside it! Then he starts singing "Close Every Door to Me" from Joseph, very quiet but maudlin FROM INSIDE THE CLOSET. I just stand there laughing, partly from embarrassment, partly relief, and partly 'cause it's really funny that he was still in the closet by himself, singing. I started laughing and couldn't really stop. (I think I was having a little bit of a breakdown/hysteria like we used to in social studies, 'member?) So I just slid down the wall and was sitting on the floor, laughing out of control (almost crying). I think it was suddenly all too much—*Joseph* ending, being so confused about M.M., slow dancing with him, etc.

So then Katie comes and sits next to me and starts laughing too, sort of fake/theatrical laughing like the game Ha Ha, and Wes joins us (he's fake laughing too), and then Michael comes out and starts in too, till we're all laughing hysterically at the top of our lungs—only I *really* was, and they were being theatrical. Tears started coming out of my eyes, so I had to get up and go to the bathroom so no one would see, and I had to get a hold of myself. Myrna's dad came right after that and took us home and I haven't seen M.M. since we were laughing on the floor like a bunch of nut jobs!

SO!

Yes, we slow danced.

Yes, he dragged me into a dark closet to be alone with me.

Nothing else happened except I panicked and he probably thinks I don't like him.

But what about Shelly, anyway?

I'm glad nothing happened. But I'm also sad. I mean, he seems like a player, right? If he has a girlfriend but stuffs other girls into closets? What does it mean? I'm hopelessly devoted to a player. AND I'll never see him because we're not in rehearsals anymore together.

Flup.

Red balloon baking in the sun.

Shriveling.

OK, Beans on Toast, see you at lunch. We're all meeting on the wall, yes?

~Cisco

@ @ @

Dear Cisco,

OK, OK, try not to pee in your pants, but I heard something that's gonna blow your mind! Flap your brain! Knock off your pantaloons! OK, I'll say it already—I overheard Madison and Alanna in English and guess what? Michael Maddix and Shelly ARE broken up!! Apparently that popular group is planning an overnight trip to Pajaro Dunes over winter break (with Joey Caccione's family in their beach house), and they were saying how things were going to be weird because Shelly was really mad at Michael but they'd already all made plans to be in the same house together for this trip. Madison and Alanna were moaning about having to act mad at Michael for Shelly's sake because they really like him and want the trip to be fun! So they are broken up AND that *means* when's he smushed you in that closet he was probably a free man and wasn't making a move on you behind his girlfriend's back!

Oh Cisco, you should do something to show that you like him! I'm sure he thinks you *don't* after you deserted him in the coat closet! Alone with the coats! Oh I wish we could have an immediate emergency meeting of Flirt Club to figure out how to remedy this. But I have to study tonight and tomorrow like a mad woman for the rest of my finals. I can't believe this development is happening NOW, with only three days of school until winter break! Errrg, how frustrating! Here is my suggestion to you, my dearest friend: Go to him! Now! Go unbosom yourself (I don't mean flash him). Tell him of your lifelong love! Or if your tongue should quaver and fail in fear, pat him on the bottom! Spank him lightly but with lust and good humor!

Now my friend, go!

P.S. I heard the math final is hard. I have it next. I'm afeared, Cisco, afeared.

–P.P.S. Go!

Oh Bean!

I wish I could be so bold as to unbosom myself . . . or even say hi on the rare occasions that I pass him in the hall. But I can't! I'm still **as shy as a doorknob.** But oh. My. Gump. I am THRILLED to hear that you-know-who was no longer together with you-know-who when he stuffed me into the closet. This is a very interesting development—VERY, VERY interesting indeed. I couldn't do Flirt Club either— I'm *way* behind on studying 'cause of *Joseph* and general procrastination. Do you know it's been almost a month since we had an official meeting? Unacceptable! Though we did all see each other almost every day during *Joseph* :) Maybe we can do Flirt Club over vacation? Both Myrna and Lisa will be going away BUT they'll both be back by the 31st. SO, maybe we could have Flirt Club AND a little celebration on New Year's Eve? We could probably do it at my house. Whatcha think, my little cuff link?

Quietly squealing in my pants,

~Cisco

Cisco,

Thas purrrfect.

Brain gon. Esploded in Math. Very, very hard finul.

Slowlee dying in my pantz,

~Ben

~~~~~~

<u>Minutes for New Year's Eve Meeting of Flirt Club (Official Meeting #5)</u>

Present: Annie (Scribe), Ariane, Lisa, Myrna, and Izzy (EVERY-ONE!!)

Instead of our usual meeting structure of

☆ ideas

☆ reports

☆ practice session

we devoted the whole meeting to brainstorming about Izzy's conundrum with Michael Maddix aka THE STONE FOX!! Because of his courtship-like behavior at the cast party, and the special attention he paid to Izzy during rehearsals, we all think that she must seize the moment! Or forever hold her peace! Or forever hold her peas! (says Ariane) Or forever fold her cheese! (Myrna)

Izzy's challenges:

☆ She has no classes with him. She won't see him during rehearsals anymore (no one knows when the next show is).

☆ He probably thinks she doesn't like him due to the now historic "Hurriedly Leaving the Closet," which she now regrets deeply and so do we. We all gave her one (gentle) pinch each for panicking and leaving before the LOVE OF HER LIFE could give her a smooch.

☆ Izzy is shy.

☆ And lastly, Michael Maddix is in a different group, the POPULAR group. That coat-closet thing was the chance of a lifetime. BUT. Let's not harp. That's why Flirt Club is the powerful, covert, underground organization that it is—to resolve seemingly impossible riddles.

Brainstorming Session:

☆ One of us could have a party and invite him. A drama party, sort of like the cast party but unchaperoned. THIS SOUNDS FUN!! BUT IMPOSSIBLE. We all have hovering parents that never go away and leave us on our own.

☆ We all HEARTILY suggested that she walk up to him during lunch and start a conversation.

We all volunteered to script a scintillating conversation for her and rehearse it with her, but she feels too shy. Collective sigh. Verging on a groan. No amount of convincing seemed to help her make the leap.

☆ BUT she did like the idea of all of us sitting near him (and thus the popular group) at lunch and trying to start some sort of action/communication most likely by throwing some food or crumpled-up paper in his general direction. (Sometimes I think this should be called "Throw Club" instead of "Flirt Club.")

☆ Myrna was all for the whole dropping something in his general vicinity approach (although this hasn't been a successful technique for her or any of us at this point!). She was certain that if he does like her he'd jump on the opportunity to retrieve her belongings.

☆ Lisa said that she thought she may be able to get a hold of M.M.'s e-mail for Izzy 'cause her brother and M.M. are in the same soccer league. But Isabelle *cringed* at this idea. She said it'd be stalkerish, plus there's her general skittishness/discomfort around technology.

☆ Ariane suggested a note—charming, a little flirtatious—wherein Izzy expresses regret at having jumped out of the closet and gives Michael Maddix aka the Stone Fox the impression that she may be interested, but nothing so bold as "I like you, do you like me?" Izzy seemed like she might be able to do the note thing IF, and this is a big IF, we can come up with the perfect

    ☆   oh so casual
    ☆   but flirtatious
    ☆   charming
    ☆   but not too charming (can't appear to be try-ing too hard)
    ☆   fun, funny
        note.

Then we spent an hour or so composing notes. Here were some of our best efforts:

Dear Michael,
Meet me in the janitor's closet between 3rd and 4th period.
Love,
Izzy Mercer-Crow
P.S. Just kidding! Just wishing I'd stayed in Mrs. P.'s coat closet for a few more seconds. ;)

Dear Michael,

Sorry to have ended our slow dance in the coat closet so abruptly the other night. What you don't know is that I'm totally claustrophobic! Perhaps you could you drag me into a small enclosed space again and help me try to cure it.

;)

Love,

Izzy Mercer-Crow

Dear Michael,

Sorry I ended our slow dance the other night by jumping out of the closet and collapsing on the floor in hysterics. I guess your intoxicating man-smell was too much for me, and I temporarily lost my senses. Now I have regained them.

;)

~Izzy aka the dancing, singing corn

(WE ALL LOVE THIS EXCEPT IZZY—SHE'S AFRAID HE WON'T GET THAT THE INTOXI-CATING MAN-SMELL BIT IS A JOKE—*Is* it a joke? *That* is the question!!)

Dear Michael,

Sorry I ended our slow dance the other night by jumping out of the closet. I panicked because I thought you were Shelly Scott's boyfriend and I've had a crush on you since kindergarten. Basically you've been the love of my life since I played Rapunzel's mother and you played my 5-year-old husband and I had to sing to you about fetching me radishes.

Love,

Izzy

This one is not a real option, it was written by Izzy for therapeutic purposes only!!

Anyhoo, the first three were the best ones that we came up with, the ones she is considering dropping in his locker. She said she needs to think about it and who can blame her?

In Conclusion: Our mission, if we should choose to accept it, is ~

1. Sit near Michael Maddix and his group Monday during lunch. We will throw some things at him/in his general direction and see if we can get into a food fight or something so him and Izzy have a chance to interact.

2. If, and that's a BIG if, Izzy feels comfortable, she will slip a note into his locker as soon as

possible. We all feel that time is of the essence here. One of those popular girls is sure to throw herself at him, if they haven't already, so Izzy needs to CARPE DIEM!! Or as Lisa says, CARPET DIEM!

This is our initial plan of covert attack.

May we live long and prosper.

Before we finished, Lisa gave everyone their Christmas/Hanukkah presents, these totally cute beanies SHE KNITTED HERSELF! They all match in style (adorable puff balls on top!) but are different colors.

And lastly we all put on our matching beanies and squinched our eyes shut and crossed our fingers for exactly 10 seconds while fervently wishing that Michael didn't get back together with Shelly at the popular group's Pajaro Dunes Getaway.

Thus ends the 5th official meeting of Flirt Club—Long Live Flirt Club!

And now! Onto the portion of the evening involving Merry Making and Revelry!!

Which is dorkspeak for pizza and DVDs.

9

French Fries Rain Down Randomly
All Over the Popular People

~~~~~~

Izzy's Journal

Well, I think I'm going to have to drop a note in M.M.'s locker. The throwing-things-at-lunch plan sort of worked but with no spectacular results. We sat on the picnic table next to the popular people's table. I was pretty nervous, my hands were sweating, etc. I felt self-conscious, like maybe the popular people would think we were trying to cozy up to their group so we could be part of it. Usually people leave a wide berth around that group during lunch. It's weird, really, if you think about it. Like the popular people are landowners, the landlords of a handful of picnic tables in Center Quad that no one dares to sit at during snack break and lunch. Anyway, we sat closer than most people usually do. I had my back to their table because I was blushing like a beet. And Annie-Bean, who's facing me, says through her teeth, "He's here, he just sat down with Scott Broderson and Mick Jones, *not* Shelly." And she gave me a "high one," which is like a high five but with just one finger. It's a covert, secret-agent move we made up for times when sneaki-ness is called for. After we ate peaceably for about five minutes, Myrna says super-spy-quiet, "OK, Izzy, you have an open shot at Michael, carpet diem!" And I couldn't do it, I froze. It's like the popular people have an invisible force field around them and the greatest social faux pas in the universe is to breech that invisible boundary. Even if it's only with a French fry. Even though Michael and I talked a million times during *Joseph*. So we all sat there talking through our teeth. Annie's all, "Do it, do it *now!* He's right behind you!" and I'm all, "No I can't, *I can't!*" Lisa goes "You have to *do something quick*—they're almost fin-ished with their lunches," and I'm just sitting there going "No" through my teeth. Finally Myrna goes, "He's done! He's done with his lunch, carpet diem!!" and I just chew the same bite of French fry that's been in my mouth for the last five min-utes. Finally, Myrna goes, "OK, *OK,* I'll do it. Will you let me throw a French fry at him? He won't know who did it. Can I?" and before I answer, she grabs, like, eight of my French fries and HURLS them (WITH A LOUD GRUNT!!) at the next table.

I turn to watch in horror as the french fries rain down ran-domly all over the popular people.

Not one of them hits Michael Maddix.

The popular table suddenly gets really quiet, and they all turn to stare at us. I turn so red and bend my face down to cover my fries so they don't think I did it. Cheeky, cheeky Myrna just smiles and waves at them, and she told me later that

Mia and Madison waved back and some of the guys chuckled. So there I am with my face in my fries and Myrna hisses, "OK, gimme the rest of those." I'm like, "What?" She can't be serious. I'm terrified she's *launching our social death.* "Try to hit Michael this time," I hiss, and she hisses back, "I'm gonna hit him with a French fry if it kills me." So one by one she starts launching fries.

The first one hits Joey Caccione in the head and lands right in front of *Mick Jones.* He throws it back at us and it hits me in the back. I turn around and he shrugs and smiles. Things are getting interesting. The next two fries hit the Designated Target: one hits Michael's shoulder and he doesn't notice, and the other hits him smack-dab in the *forehead.* The forehead fry does the trick. He picks it up, looks at us with an unreadable expression on his face. Myrna shrugs and he looks directly at me. This is all making me so nervous I am sweating and feel like I may start to giggle uncontrollably or pee in my pants. He gets up. Walks over to our table. (I distinctly saw Madison roll her eyes as he walked over.) He stands right next to me and says into my eyes, "Excuse me, I think one of you young ladies dropped this." I reach for it and he presses it into my hand and holds my hand while he's doing it. Then he smiles and walks away.

Oh blessed greasy, dirt-encrusted French fry! Oh blessed Myrna, crazy French fry launcher! So, it kind of worked. I got to hold his hand for three seconds. But then . . . nada! Now what? Nothing else happened after that. No more communication between the tables. And, of course, I didn't see him again all day 'cause I never do. So it may be time for the note. I'd like to wait a few days to see if something happens naturally—maybe he'll come up to me or something. My Sisters of the Corn think I should act fast, carpet diem and all that. It's just I'm so shy at the thought of putting a flirty note in his locker! But it's true that one of those popular girls may snap him up right away. But he'd have to want to be snapped, right?

Dear Cisco,

Well, poo on a stick. The play Mrs. P. chose isn't a musical. It's a good one—*To Kill a Mockingbird*—but there's no singing or dancing. Maybe you'll still want to try out? You're a good actress! I know dancing and singing are more your cup of tea, but . . . *please?* I can't imagine going to rehearsals without my Sisters of the Corn, aka Flirt Club, aka Secret Agents. Assuming, of course, that I get a part. (I can't assume I'll be in it just 'cause I want to.) I'm really bummed it's not a musical. But Mrs. P. said that she thought a drama would stretch and develop our abilities. She's right. But flup stretching and developing. Auditions are in two weeks. We have to perform a dramatic monologue and read from the script for the auditions. Please consider, just consider, doing it? I'd help you every day with your monologue if you want.

In other sad news, I bet M.M. won't try out because the main reason he was in *Joseph* was because of his voice, right? Does he like dramatic acting? If he tried out, would you? I wish I had a crush on someone. Now that I broke up with Enrique's ear and Sean dumped me (or dumped his interest in me), I'm a little bored in the romance department. It's nice to have

Wups gotta go, incoming floating eyeball spacecraft

write back,
Bean

P.S. I left a pop quiz for you in your locker.

Beanie Baby,

I'm so glad you wrote me, I'm so bored. I took your pop quiz and think I did a very excellent job. I'll put it in your locker for you. We had a test today in Science and I finished super fast and now I have half an hour to fill. Hmmm...I'll think about auditioning. I'm NOT a good actress. I get too nervous. My limbs shake, my voice quakes if everyone is looking at me. I like being in a group, like in *Joseph*, a posse of corn. I like singing. Maybe I'll practice with you and just see how it goes. Nothing's happening on the M.M. front. It's been three days since he squished a greasy French fry into my hand. It may be time to do the note thing 'cause I don't know how the flup else I'll ever communicate with him again. I mean, we can't throw food at him at lunch every day, that's too dorky for words.

That blank space represents me imagining a lifetime committed to hurling food at M.M. every lunch hour. That is a life of sad geekdom I cringe to think of. Sigh . . . Oh I'm so smitten. Crap! It's as bad as when he played my husband in *Rapunzel*. Did you know that because M. and I played husband and wife in *Rapunzel*, in my little kindergarten mind, I assumed he would *really* be my husband when I grew up? I thought it was a sort of betrothal, and I was thrilled and relieved to have the husband-finding business out of the way at such a young age.

(That was another moment of silence to ponder in disbelief my incredible dorkiness, which has apparently been with me since kindergarten!!!)

We're meeting at the usual place, sí? My little tortilla?

Love,
Cisco

P.S. Love your shirt.

Dear Cisco,

You *are* a good actress. You played Rapunzel in kindergarten and did a smashing job! You didn't have stage fright then, did you?

YES. YOU MUST DROP A NOTE IN M.M.'S LOCKER. I'll do it for you if you want!

Love,
Bean

~~~~~~

Izzy's Journal

Well, the week's over and I didn't drop a note for Michael Maddix or do anything to flirt with him 'cause I never see him. I miss *Joseph* rehearsals so much! Enrique has sort of been ignoring me in English too, which is sort of a relief and sort of a bummer. I still feel like it would be cruel to Annie if anything were to happen with Enrique even though she's mostly over Sean. And I guess I've been so crushed out on Michael since *Joseph* that I haven't really been thinking about Enrique. I'm a one-man woman even when my man is imaginary. Enrique probably just got tired of hitting his head on a brick wall (me), or he likes someone else now. It's weird, I feel kind of sad, like we broke up or something. I'm crazy. But I sort of miss him pulling on my hair and trying to make me laugh. But it's good, too, 'cause now I don't have to feel guilty for Annie's sake. I've decided that I'm for sure gonna do the note-in-Michael's-locker thing. If he doesn't like me, it won't be too weird 'cause I won't have confessed undying love or anything.

I'm going to do it Monday!

CARPET DIEM!!!! After writing about 50 different notes I decided to use one of the ones we came up with at Flirt Club:

Dear Michael,
Sorry to have ended our slow dance in the closet so abruptly the other night. What you don't know is that I'm totally claustrophobic! Perhaps you could drag me into the art supply closet sometime and help me try to cure it.
;)
Sincerely,
Izzy Mercer-Crow

I feel pretty good about it—it's flirty (too flirty? I re-read it to Annie over the phone; she said the flirtiness is good.) But I felt safe suggesting the art-supply closet 'cause it's always locked. I've written it on a small piece of binder paper ripped off from a regular piece. That way I think it looks casual, sort of off-hand. Not too . . . I don't know, desperate. At first I wrote it on that perfumed lavender stationary that Grandma gave me, with the little matching lavender envelopes. But then ripped it into a million shreds! That would have been so dorky and earnest. I do earnestly care for him. BUT, I just want to appear playful and flirty, not stalkerish. I know a girl in a Jane Austen book would have definitely used the lavender stationery, BUT THESE ARE DIFFERENT DAYS! No one in a Jane Austen novel would get shoved into a closet as part of a courtship, that's for sure!! He would be considered the worst sort of cad and to be shunned just for pulling me into a closet to be kissed. I shouldn't shun him should I? IS he a cad? What a great word! The dictionary says it means: "a man or boy whose behavior is not gentlemanly."

I'll tell you who was a cad, and that is Sean Higgins.

@ @ @

Oh Bean,

I did it! I shoved the note in M.M.'s locker between 1st and second period! And I can't concentrate! Mrs. Bermoth is going on about participles and verboliums or I have no idea. I am writing on the oh-so-sly with shaking and sweaty hands. Absolutely no joke. Here: ⬤ this is a smudge print of thumb sweat. Sorry for the grossness but I have to demonstrate my terror. Why. Did. I. Do. It.

?

Why did I put the note in his locker?
I want to duck and cover! I just want to curl up on the floor

under my desk, cover the tender back of my neck with my hands, and stay there all day. Do you think it would be weird for me to do an earthquake drill all day with no one else participating? I feel

Ah! had to go for a bit, Mrs. Bermoth actually called on me! The nerve! Trying to teach me! Make me a smarter person! Boo! Anyhoo, now I'm writing you from the bathroom stall & have to run.

Pray for me.

For my writhing soul.
Cisco

Cicso,

Brave girl! Good brave girl! Just think of it like this. When you are 96 years old and on your deathbed, you won't have to wonder what would have happened if you had had the courage to do something about your lifelong crush on Michael Maddix. Even if he doesn't respond, you've had the courage to stand by your own heart!

SWELLING MUSIC!!!

No, I mean it. High five!

OK, please come over after school if you can, I think we should start practicing our dramatic monologues? Please don't change your mind! I know you haven't said you'll audition, but you did say you'd consider it and practice a monologue with me. Think of it this way—it will help you take your mind off the Michael Maddix situation. I've got monologues from *Antigone, Romeo and Juliet, Our Town*, and a whole book Mrs. P. lent me that I haven't looked through yet.

Love,
Your very own Bean

Bean,

Yes, yes, I'll come over. My hands have been sweating all day. No note or sign from You Know Who. I don't even know if he's been to his locker. I don't know his habits. Someone should write a book: "The Locker-Going Habits of the Eighth-Grade North American Boy."

Love,
Cisco Cisco Panties-in-a-Twisto

10

A Flurry of Notes

Bean,

Still no note or sign from the Stone Fox yet. That was fun yesterday. It did help distract me. I'm getting into my monologue. Tennessee Williams rocks. I mean, Tennessee Williams flarps. I have to read *Suddenly Last Summer* so my monologue makes more sense in my own mind. We should rent it too, like your mom was saying, though I know I'll be intimidated by Elizabeth Taylor's acting ability. You are so good! Your monologue almost made me cry. I bet you get Scout. I mean Katie Chethik is also a really good dramatic actress and I know she wants the role of Scout, but she has huge bosoms! Not that there's anything wrong with huge bosoms! But Scout's supposed to be a kid and you are much more lithe and petite. I can't imagine a Scout with giant buzoomgas! Can you? I bet Andrew Pease gets Jem, he's the smallest drama guy. And I know he's still ticked off at not getting Joseph (we all thought he was a shoo-in until the Stone Fox rocked our world!). I bet

Mrs. P. gives him either Atticus or Jem. He deserves it, he's good.

Write me back as often as you can today, I need a flurry of notes to take my mind off things!

Love,
Cisco

Cisco,

Yes, I agree I'd make a perfect Scout. Hope Mrs. P. sees it that way. I mean, they could bind Katie's bosoms to make her look less womanly, right? I know Mrs. P. thinks my main talent lies in comedic acting and Katie's lie in dramatic, so I'm gonna have to really prove myself. Oh guess what—Myrna, Lisa, and Ariane are trying out too! Yippee! I just wish there were more parts for girls in *Mockingbird*.

Love,
Bean

P.S. Let the flurry begin.

Dear Izzy,

Myrna here. I hear you need a flurry of notes to distract you, so I'm writing you a note. Hmmm . . . I hear you did the deed, the dropping of the note in M******'s lock**.

You're very b****!

I am trying out for *To Kill a Mockingbird*!! I know I will be a townsperson, so don't worry about the competition.

Love,
M

Dear Izzy,

Hi. Good luck with you know who.

Sincerely,
Lisa

P.S. Sorry my note is so short & boring, I am not the greatest note writer!

Dear Isabelle Mercer-Crow,

We here at the NASA Space Facility have chosen you to participate in our space program! You have all the qualities we look for when recruiting astronauts. Do you like whirling, antigravity amusement park–like rides that are designed for science, not pleasure? We thought so! We hope you will come for a tour of our facilities and—

Whoops, sorry Miss Mercer-Crow, our computer has made an error. You have NOT been chosen for NASA Space programs.

Our bad!

Love,
NASA
(aka Ariane)

P.S. Hang in there, space-kitten!
P.P.S. Not that you wouldn't be a GREAT astronaut if that's what you wanted to do!

Dear Izzy,
Hi again.
From,
Lisa again
(still not the greatest note writer)

Dear Cisco,
You wanted a flurry . . . well, ask and you shall receive!
Hope your tremors and sweats have abated a bit. Remember, you rock! I mean, you flarp. Here's a collage I made for you during free period.

Love,
Bean

Izzy,

Let's have Flirt Club this Saturday.

Love,
Ariane

Dear I***,

It turns out I really like using the stars in place of letters, because we are Secret A***** and all, it is imp****** that I be tricky tricky dicky. I hope the fl**** of notes is help*** to distract you from the S**** F** situation.

Love,
Myrna
I mean M****

Dear Izzy,

This is the last boring note from me, I promise!

Love,
Lisa

◎ ◎ ◎

Izzy's Journal

That was so sweet of the girls to shower me with a "flurry" of notes today in my locker to help distract me. Even though it made me feel good, it was also TORTURE! 'Cause every time I opened one of their notes, I would get all shaky inside and my hands would sweat because I DESPERATELY hoped it was from Michael! And it never was! So it was great but also sort of torturous!! I'd never tell them that, of course. But I still loved it—I'll save the notes and put them in our scrapbook as a memento.

Jeez, I dropped the note in Michael's locker yesterday early in the day, so basically it's been two full days and no response. I mean, if I really liked someone I'd respond quicker than that. I did get a hang-up on the family landline last night, but that happens all the time at our house, and there's no way he'd call—he doesn't even have my number. Though I guess my home phone is listed.

We ate lunch in the cafeteria yesterday and today to stay warm, so I actually haven't see M.M. at all. Except once I saw his back way ahead of me down the hall for a second before he turned a corner. I'm glad it was his back, though; I don't think I could face him! He obviously doesn't like me and was just flirting for fun. I don't know why I ever thought he would. He's one of the most popular guys in school. I'd say him, Mick Jones, and Sam Lopez are the top three. Oh, and Joey Caccione, so top four, really. What was I thinking? I have a terrible lump in my stomach. Maybe I'll be sick tomorrow. That'd be great. I could sit and watch videos and forget that I exist.

I'm sure I'll be fine. I have an iron constitution.

Flup.

Dear Bean,

Still nothing. I'm sunk.

Love,
Cisco

Dear Bean,

Still nothing and the day's almost over. It's been three days. I'm going to enter the witness protection program & get a new face. A better one.

Love,
Cisco

Dear Cisco,

You have a wonderful face.

Shush about changing it. Did you hear that Abby McDougal

got a nose job over the summer? I wonder if it's true. Her nose always seemed fine to me.

Anyway, it's really like two days 'cause he may not have gotten it the day you dropped it in his locker.

Love,
Bean

P.S. I made you another collage.
P.P.S. Your face IS wonderful just like it is.

Bean,

OK, it's been 4 days and still nothing. The week's practically over, along with my former life, where I had a shred of dignity. Why? Why did I do it? Can we have lunch in one of the bathroom stalls tomorrow? Not really, but I do feel the need to hide my face forevermore. You're probably right about there being other fish in the sea and that Enrique may still like me—all that nice stuff you said at lunch—but for some reason, I only want this fish. Just this one.

Love,
Your ever-loving Mer-blob

Cisco,

You are not a Mer-blob or a blob of any sort. I understand about the M.M. fish.

Come over after school and I can show you this video I found online of the amazing barrel fish—ITS HEAD IS A TRANSLUCENT DOME, and its eyeballs ARE INSIDE ITS TRANSLUCENT HEAD! *And* we can watch the video of *Joseph* my dad took.

Love,
Bean

Cisco,

Flup. I realized after I dropped that last note in your locker a minute ago that you may not want to watch *Joseph* 'cause of M.M. being the star and all—whoops.

Sorry, I'm the blob, a big blob of sorry.

Bean

Bean,

Shhh, silly, don't be a sorry blob, I'd love to watch *Joseph* with you and see the amazing barrel fish. You're a great friend.

Let us not speak of blobs any further.

See you after school,

Izzy

~~~~~~

Izzy's Journal

What I didn't tell Annie is that today after science I saw Michael in the hall in the distance talking to Shelly Scott. He was kind of close to her, leaning toward her with one arm propped against the lockers. They weren't actually touching. They looked friendly. I don't know how friendly. But I felt my stomach drop. In one way it would be good if they were back together because then if he ignores me from here on out, I can blame it on them getting back together. And not go around feeling like a big embarrassed slug. I do feel like a slug—not fat or anything, but so exposed. Is a slug a snail without a shell? That's how I feel . . . like a snail without a shell.

I don't know about this whole carpet diem thing. I mean, that's all fine and good for the Sisters of the Corn to say and all, but they didn't just risk rejection from one of the most popular boys in school.

Bean! Bean bean bean bean!

I got a note from YOU KNOW WHO! My hands are shaking—I'm standing in front of your locker, writing on the metal surface super close so no one can see! His note says to meet him after school at his locker!!! Oh my gosh! *Why did he wait FIVE DAYS to respond?*

I'm so nervous, I'm gonna barf!

Love,
Cisco

Cisco,

Oh my God! Don't barf! Ahhhh! I can't believe it! Except I can believe it 'cause you're so great! OK, OK, make sure he doesn't just try to use you for sex! Unless you *want* to be used! Maybe your note shouldn't have said anything about going back into a closet! Oh dear, did we steer you wrong? Oh dear, why am I turning into such a mom all of a sudden! Sorry! Like he's gonna try to have sex with you in the hall or something!

This is excellent news! See you at the wall for lunch.

Love,
Bear

P.S. Don't forget Flirt Club tomorrow!

Izzy's Journal Friday Evening

Oh dear journal, guess what? I didn't barf! But I can hardly write 'cause I feel so jittery/excited! So. After 7th period, I walked over to M.M.'s locker after I'd been to my own. (Kind of quickly 'cause his locker is pretty far from mine but not *too* quickly—I didn't want to be too early and be there waiting for him when he arrived; that'd be SO dorky.) So I walk over there and I feel like I can't get my breath and he's there just leaning against his locker, chewing a straw or something. When he sees me coming, he grins real big, and I do, too. He goes, "How's it going, Corn?" And I go, "Good," and nod a bunch of times and look at the red concrete floor. Which was not as red as my face, I'm sure. I just keep nodding at the ground—I have absolutely no cleverness under pressure. Luckily he does! So he goes, "Did you change your hair?" And my eyes just about fell out of my head! 'Cause I did, I parted it way on one side 'cause I thought it looked sexy and all Lauren Bacall. Nobody even noticed— BUT HE DID!! "Yeah," I said, and laughed. And HE THEN PROCEEDED to grab a strand, tuck it behind my ear, and say, "It looks nice." I mumbled thanks and felt like I might fall down. He either really likes me or is one smooth mother-flupper.

He goes, "I miss rehearsals," and I nod and we're totally looking in each other's eyes, and I say, "Me too." So, he goes, "Are you REALLY claustrophobic? Or are you maybe a little *Michael*-phobic?" He's teasing, but I can tell he's kind of nervous too.

I say, "No, I really am claustrophobic, terribly. Once my cousin put a sleeping bag over my head and I freaked out so bad—crying and shaking for, like, half an hour—that my dad finally gave me hot water with brandy in it to calm me down." "Really?" he said, and I go, "Yeah." (I couldn't believe I'd gotten that many words out!) And he goes, "Are you walking home?" And I go, "Yeah." He says, "Cool, can I walk you?" and I'm like, "Isn't it out of your way?" and he goes, "Just a little."

So he walked me home!! And it was fun! And talking was pretty easy. We talked about *Joseph* and all the silly plays we were in in elementary school, including *The Choice*. Oh my God, I'd forgotten all about *The Choice*. That was such a stupid play! I was the wife and he was the husband (again!), and he'd forgotten his lines during our one and only performance in the multipurpose room in front of the whole school. He'd been a bit of a slacker about his lines and kept forgetting them. Once he just kept saying the same line over and over and pacing back and forth on stage. I was laughing so hard I acted like I was crying (which made sense for my character). So I sat there laugh-crying into my hands, and he paced and paced, repeating himself like a broken record until finally the director pulled the curtains closed as if the play was over. (IT WASN'T!!) They finally opened the curtains again when we'd gotten a handle on ourselves. How could I have forgotten that? Maybe it was too painful to remember! But we laughed so hard about it on the way home.

I really like him. He's not all snobby or anything now that he's one of "the Popular People." He's the same bundle of joy he always was. Sigh! ANYWAY, when we got to my house we stood awkwardly at the end of my walkway and neither of us said anything for a while. It was embarrassing but not too bad. It seems like he may actually be shy too. And then he goes, "Thanks for letting me walk you home, madam," and he kisses the back of my hand and bows a courtly bow! Like he knew my fixation with Jane Austen, etc.! And then he walked off!

Oh, it was dreamy and I'm all buzzy and melty! Of course, I ran inside and called Annie right away and told her everything!! She thinks maybe I should have invited him in . . . but our house is messy and my annoying sister was home. I don't think I could have dealt with being hostess in that moment! I'll never sleep tonight! Ever!

11

Destiny Calling

~~~~~~

Flirt Club Meeting Number Six

First order of business: to celebrate Izzy's success with Michael Maddix, the Stone Fox, himself!!

We gave three cheers—"Hip, hip, hooray!"—to Izzy! (yep, we're still dorks).

Then we gave three cheers—"Hip, hip, hooray!"—to Flirt Club as a whole for accomplishing the whole "plotting and writing the note for M.M.'s locker" mission. We really are excellent secret agents. I think we deserve a raise.

Flirt Club flarps! Even though we're dorks!

~~~~~~

NEW FLIRTING TECHNIQUES:

Well, it turns out no one has any new ones because we have plenty of old ones to grapple with. BUT we all agree that "grapple" is a great word. So we cheered—"Hip, hip, hooray!"—for "grapple," and we raised our invisible chalices!

CLINK!!

And Ariane expressed her profound wish that one of our missions should somehow include a *grappling hook*.

Hmmm. This brought about a long pause wherein we all scratched our heads for a bit.

AnyHOO!

Flirting Reports (besides Izzy's major victory
with the Stone Fox since we all know every
detail of that event!):

Myrna: Myrna successfully dropped her binder at Sam Lopez's unsuspecting feet (on them actually). After wincing and politely brushing aside her apologies, he picked it up for her and winked! Coming from Sam Lopez a wink doesn't mean that much, but we raised our invisible chalices to Myrna the Brave! *Clink, clink*! Sam Lopez is soooooo hot!

Lisa: Has nothing to report. We still toast Lisa! *Clink, clink, clink*!

Ariane: Ariane has taken to passing boys in the hall and giving them lightning-fast winks! She showed us her technique—it's astounding! Because, it's so fast you're not sure it's happened! And that way the boys are left wondering—did she wink at me or not? Does she have a facial tic?

It's good to leave them wondering, we all decided. Boys that Ariane has winked at to date:

Joey Caccione! (cheeky, cheeky Ariane!)

Sam Lopez (he seems to be a favorite target!)

Danny Rosenberg

George Plath

Toby McGuinty (He's cute—we all decided that Toby McGuinty is suddenly very cute! All that baby fat is completely gone! Where'd it go?)

Jim Henderson

Those are the ones she remembers. Crazy winking girl!

Annie (me): Nothing to report. I've been very focused on my audition monologue and studying the script for *To Kill a Mockingbird*. We all heartily agree it's excellent for a girl to be focused on her dreams and goals (not just boys). In support of that theory they all watched my audition monologue. And gave me helpful ideas. I did it five times, and by the end they said it was excellent!

Instead of a flirt practice session, we all watched the video of *Joseph* (again) together and laughed at ourselves in our dumb corn hats! But we all concluded that we looked kind of sexy in our Egyptian costumes.

In conclusion:

1. Flirt Club is working miracles, particularly the fact that the crush OF IZZY'S LIFE walked her home and kissed her hand.
2. Dropping things and throwing things seem to be fairly successful techniques for shy girls like us.
3. We kicked some ass as the chorus in *Joseph*— what passion and commitment for mere starchy vegetables!
4. Ariane is a winking ninja, and we all committed to try and master her technique.

Note: We added some more things to our Flirt Club Scrap Book/Almanac. Some of the notes from the historic "flurry of notes" that we used to try to distract Izzy. We added a picture from the school paper of the side of Toby McGuinty's head because we've all decided he's a Stone Fox and definitely a Worthy Designated Target (WDT). And we put on Ariane's strawberry lip smackers and kissed a piece of paper to seal our commitment to Flirt Club and keeping it a secret. We decided if and when any of us get boyfriends we *cannot* tell them about Flirt Club.

And lastly, before we finished, Myrna clinked her invisible fork against her invisible chalice and made an announcement. She is going to try wearing some girlier clothes versus her usual hoodies, flannels, and jeans. She said she may even get some SEXY clothes, whereafter we all went, "Oooooooo, sexy lady," etc. Then Myrna raised her chalice and cried, "But I shall never renounce flannel entirely, NEVER!" And proceeded to hug her own shirt. Then LISA had the BRILLIANT idea of designing and sewing Myrna a cute new shirt outta one of her old flannels. (I wish Lisa was my mom.) Then Myrna hugged Lisa and Ariane hugged 'em both and Izzy and I tackled them.

And thus we concluded the Sixth Official Meeting of Flirt Club in a giggle pile.

Long Live Flirt Club!

Bean!

I got a note today in my locker from M****** M*****! He invited me to a party on Saturday at Joey Caccione's! He left me his cell phone number and asked me to call him tonight. Can you believe it? I think it might be a date! I can't believe I'm invited to one of their parties! Weird beyond weird. I wish I could bring you and all the Sisters of the Corn, but since this is our first date, I don't think I can ask. If that makes you feel bad, I won't go.

Love,
Cisco

Cisco,

Nabisco! Of course you should go! AND you shouldn't even *think* of asking if you can bring the rest of us. For one thing, IT IS DEFINITELY A DATE! *And,* according to the deeply informative TV show "Blind Date," you *never* bring your friends along on a first date! Plus, it'd be too weird for you to bring all your drama geek friends to a popular party—they'd probably skin us alive and hang us in the shed to make geek-jerky. Ha-ha! Get it? *Geek*-jerky? I just made that up! Pretty funny, if I don't say so myself.

I hope you can still come over today and tomorrow to practice monologues. Auditions are in three days! I'm so afraid to hope for Scout because last time I was so sorely disappointed to be a piece of corn. (Though, of course, it was SO fun being with my corn sisters.) But I *really* hope that I don't end up a townsperson!

Love,
Bean

P.S. Agent #88, you HAVE to take pictures at the popular party with your microscopic eyeball spy camera so we can see how the other half lives. Which won't be too hard since all the girls will be moving in slow motion. Get it? You know how in all teenage movies the first shot of the popular girls is always of them walking toward the camera in slow motion, hair swinging, clothes perfect, etc.!

Bean,

Of course I'll be over after school to do monologues. Maybe I could call M.M. from your house before I go home for dinner? I'm so nervous to call him that I literally feel like I may not be able to do it!

Love,
Cisco

Cisco,

Yay! I'll see you at your locker and DO call M.M. from my house—in fact, I won't let you leave until you do. YOU CANNOT CHICKEN OUT. YOUR DESTINY IS CALLING YOU!! Brrring-brring . . .

(You say) "Hello?"

"Hello, Isabelle, this is your destiny calling, wassup?"

~Bean

P.S. It is MY Destiny to ACT. I have a flair for the DRAMATIC!

Izzy's Journal

Ahhhhh! So it's final! I'm going to a party with Michael Maddix at Joey Caccione's! I can't believe it. I just tried on everything I own and I'm pretty sure nothing is cute enough. I know the secret agents will help me though. Either lend me something or go with me to the mall on Friday. I'm so lucky; I have the best friends in the world. And now Michael has asked me to a party. I have to tell my parents—that'll be weird. God, I'm so nervous about the party. I won't really know the people—I mean, Alanna Markley and I used to be friends, but that was, like, in 3rd grade. She just looks through me these days. Oh, this is so weird. I'd give my right eyebrow if Annie could come! Maybe if Michael and I go out again (I can't believe I just wrote that!) to a party I could bring Annie. But what about the other Sisters of the Corn? Oh, this is so stressful. And wonderful.

Shoot—auditions are Friday! We can't go to the mall that day . . . maybe someone could go with me Thursday? Ahhhh! Wardrobe emergency! Talking on the phone with Michael was weird and awkward. Or I should say I was weird and awkward. He's like, "Hi, Izzy, what's up?" And I go, "Nothing!" in this chipper parakeet voice! Ugh! "Sooo," he drawls, "you wanna go to this party on Saturday with me?" I go, "Sure!" Chirp! I sounded like a terrified bird! "OK . . . cool." (He sounded really pleased though, like he thought I might say no or something!!!) So then he wrote down my address "to make sure he didn't walk up to the wrong house" and said he'd be over at 8:00 to pick me up and we could walk to Joey's 'cause it's so close to me.

The conversation was super short and I was glad 'cause I am so shy and dorky. Ugh!! Why am I that way? Annie said (I was at her house still when I called M.M.) that I sounded fine, but I think she's just being nice. Maybe when I go to the party with him someone should shoot me with a tranquilizer gun like the animals on *Wild Kingdom.* They're running, running all wild and fast and then "Thwap!" they run a little slower, then slower, until "Foomp!" they fall over and just look up helplessly as the humans hoist them onto the flatbed of a truck or tag them or whatever. I guess I wouldn't be a very interesting date though if I didn't have any muscle control and just looked up limply at Michael Maddix from the ground!

Oh my God! And FRIDAY IS AUDITION DAY! I've been forgetting about it in this whole M.M. drama (which is good because if I think about it, I become horrified!). I felt better about *Joseph* auditions because I'm pretty good at singing and dancing, but it's just plain acting this time. And doing a monologue. Ugh. I need anti-anxiety medication like Grandma takes. Life is too much right now.

BUT ALSO REALLY GOOD!

Friday

Cisco,

That outfit you got yesterday is SO cute. You're gonna knock 'em dead! You really are a stunning creature—that sea foam color makes your eyes look positively otherworldly! Totally, completely mermaidy! I'm so proud of you . . . my little Izzybella girl's all growed up! (← Where did that come from, I am so weird!) I'm so nervous about auditions today that I've had to pee once during every class so far (twice during science—I know Mr. Saunders didn't believe me and probably thinks I'm on drugs. I AM. IT'S CALLED ADRENA-LINE!). Despite practically living in the girls' bathroom, Elvis will NOT leave the building. I am compacted and gassy. I know you were waiting on the edge of your seat for an update about my poo, so there it is!

I feel really confident, though, that I did my best to prepare for this. I could do my monologue in my sleep *and* I know Scout's scenes almost by heart. THANKS TO YOU, Wonder Girl! OK, I'll see you after 7th in the Little Theater. Did you know that Chase Matthews from Cubberly High is assistant directing? He was, like, the King of Drama here at Wilbur four years ago, and now he's a bigwig high school senior who's really into directing. He's gonna be at the auditions apparently. Ariane said that Margaret P. said her sister said (oh brother!) that he's THE Stone Fox quadrupled. There's another little nerve-wracking nugget for you. (Like you need any more things to be nervous about!)

Break a leg, oh mermaid of my heart! Oh pork chop of my loin! (← What?)

Love,
Bean

12

Some Triumph and Some Trouble

~~~~~~

<u>Annie-Bean's Diary</u>

Oh my gosh, I'm so relieved (and so is my tummy, Elvis finally left the building as soon as I got home). Auditions went great!! I think my monologue kicked some serious boooo-tay. Chase spontaneously started clapping when I was done, and he hadn't clapped for anyone else. Was that wrong of him? *I* certainly didn't mind. And then they had me read Scout over and over with all the different Jems. (I think Andrew Pease was the best.) M.M. didn't try out this time. They also had Katie Chethik read as Scout over and over too (ugh.) I read for Mayella Ewell during the courtroom scene a couple of times. That would be a good part too . . . BUT I HOPE I GET SCOUT!

Izzy did well too—they didn't have her read from the script too much though, so I doubt she'll get a lead, which is just as well 'cause she doesn't really want one. I'm so excited that auditions went so well. I want this part more than ANYTHING!!

I'm happy for Izzy about the whole M.M. thing. But . . . if I'm completely honest with myself, I do feel a little weird too. I **do** wish I could go to that party . . . I'd *love* to go to a party at Joey Caccione's. And hang out with that crowd. Those guys are all SO CUTE. So, I guess I feel a little jealous. And I'm a little scared because what if she gets together with M.M. for real and then is part of that group—instead of my best friend and part of our ragtag group of oddball drama geeks??? Can she be part of both groups? Has anyone ever done that as far as I know? I guess Michael Maddix sort of straddles the drama crowd and the popular crowd . . . but he's really in the popular group.

I wish I didn't feel at all jealous, but I do a bit. I hope I'm not a bad person. This is a *super secret* agent journal entry. I better find a better place to hide my journal. If Emmet finds this and teases me or—God forbid—tells anyone, I'd have to kill him. NO ONE CAN EVER READ THIS.

I pray to the god of small-time middle-school plays that I may be Scout.

I pray to the god of the dark red concrete hallways at Wilbur that I may be Scout.

I pray to the god of Mrs. Pearson's right-hand top desk drawer (where it's rumored she keeps the cast lists!) that I may be Scout.

I pray to the god of the tattered stage-right curtain in the Little Theater that I may be Scout.

I pray to the god that lives in the bottom of Mrs. P.'s always-sticky coffee cup that I may be Scout!

Amen.

Tomorrow, the girls and I are going to go to Izzy's in the afternoon and help her get ready for the party. Oh, it'll be fun! Mostly. It may be a little like getting Cinderella ready for the ball but not getting to go myself. But the girls and I are going to go to Ariane's afterward and watch her *Gypsy* DVD. Boy I wish I could be in *that* show. But they'd probably never do it as a school production 'cause of the burlesque numbers. I hear the Palo Alto Community Theater is doing a musical in the Spring JUST for teenagers (no grown-ups or kiddies) AND they may do *Godspell*. That's what Chase Matthews said, and he is the king of the land and my heart so he should know. That would be SO FUN! Basically I'm gonna try out no matter what show they do. Community theater plays are always better than school plays. No offense to Mrs. P., who is the coolest grown-up in the history of the world.

@ @ @

Izzy's Journal Saturday night

Tonight was SO fun! And a little bit horrible! The party was NOT fun, but hanging out with Michael was. I actually, miracle of all miracles, felt pretty OK with Michael when it was just him and I walking to Joey's. And when we first got there we just sat on the porch for a while talking and all the nauseous nervousness that I'd been feeling all day just faded as we talked. I think being on stage in *Joseph* has helped me get over stage fright in REAL-LIFE situations too. He sat close to me on the porch with his thigh touching mine—Gulp! SO much better than popping Mrs. Healy's fuchsias.

People (Madison, Mia, Cathy, Annette, ALL THOSE GIRLS!!!) kept arriving. And they were all polite and said hi to me. Then we went inside and that's when it was a little awful. Joey's parents were out of town (I'd assumed in my geek-dom that they'd be there). Michael went to get me a beer, and I hate beer but was too shy to say, so I just held it without drinking. We didn't really talk 'cause the music was loud and he kept talking to his friends who I didn't know, and I was too shy to participate in the conversation.

Then Mia grabbed Michael up by the elbow and dragged him away into another room, and I was left sitting on the couch alone for half an hour! Maybe it wasn't that long, but it felt like forever! All the popular girls were across the room in a clump, and all the boys were in the kitchen playing some loud drinking game. And I have no idea where Mia and Michael were. Shelly Scott was *not* there, thank goodness. The clump of popular girls just totally ignored me. They did glance over at me sometimes but not in a mean way. Once Alanna Markley even smiled at me. She was the only one though. I just sat there looking at *Field and Stream* magazine like it was the most fascinating thing in the whole world, FEELING MORE EMBARRASSED THAN I EVER HAVE IN MY WHOLE LIFE. Even more than when snot exploded out of my nose for Michael's eyes only! If I could have crawled inside my own stomach and disguised myself as a couch pillow, I would have.

Finally, Michael and Mia came back and he plopped down next to me and said, "Sorry about that." I said it was OK even though I was kind of miffed and was feeling like I might cry. He seemed different after that, a little distracted or something, and I wondered what Mia had talked to him about but he didn't say. He asked if any of the girls had talked to me, and I said no and he said, "Bitches!" And he HELD MY HAND and pulled me off the couch and pulled me smack-dab in the middle of the girls AND PUT HIS ARM AROUND ME! And said, "This is Izzy," and he introduced me to all the girls, as if I don't know everyone and their names frontward and backward!!

Then they were polite enough, and Alanna said, "I know Izzy, I've known Izzy since preschool." Madison and Mia were the only ones who were kind of cold. They didn't even smile. But then I didn't have to deal with them anymore because Michael pulled me outside on the back porch and we talked. Then, after a long time of just talking and sitting, he kissed me!!! It was amazing. No tongue (yet!), and I was relieved 'cause I'd never done that and I didn't want to do it wrong! So we talked and kissed nice little kisses and talked more. THEN we did kiss with tongues! And it was fine. Somehow, my tongue knew what to do all on its own—yay for my tongue! I like it! Oh goodness I like Michael so much I feel like I'm gonna pull my hair out.

We didn't stay at the party too long. He asked if I wanted to walk around, and I said yes. He said he loved walking around at night and looking at people's houses with lights glowing, that he could do it forever. So could I! Before we left, though, Annette Angelo came up to me while Michael was saying good-bye to the boys. She linked her arm through mine and said, "Izzy, you're a cool chick," all slurry. She was drunk! "You seem nice," she whisper/giggled. "You seem like YOU are not a bitch!" And she looked over at Madison on the word "bitch"! I was like, "Ummmm, thanks." She laughed and said, "You should hang with us sometime again, OK?" I said sure.

I'm glad Michael didn't get drunk—that would have been weird. So he and I spent about TWO HOURS walking around in old Palo Alto where all those really nice old houses with beautiful gardens are. Just talking and sometimes quiet, BUT ALWAYS HOLDING HANDS!! And then he walked me home and, like a gentleman, kissed me on the cheek and then gave me one more soft kiss on the mouth and said he'd call me.

!!!!!!!!!!!!!!!!!!!!!!!!!

I really can't believe this. I love spending time with him! That popular people party wasn't so great though. In my opinion, the drama people are way more fun. It seems like maybe the popular people drink so they can loosen up and act as free as the drama people do all the time. I don't know. Of course, I'm prejudiced. I love my friends; they were so nice to come over and help me get ready. We played Big Booty and "This Is a Hat" for fun and to help me keep my nerves under control, just like we did backstage before every show. I can't wait to see the girls tomorrow—they're coming over, not for an official Flirt Club meeting, just to hear all about the party and hang out. Except Lisa can't :(Her mom is taking her shopping for a winter coat.

I wonder if it's hard for Annie to hear about my love life since the whole Sean debacle and her breaking up with Enrique's ear. (I can't believe I *have* a love life!)

CAST LIST FOR *TO KILL A MOCKINGBIRD*
Atticus Finch: Toby McGuinty
Jem Finch: Andrew Pease
Scout Finch: Annie Myers
Mayella Violet Ewell: Myrna Mendez
Calpurnia: Katie Chethik
Boo Radley: Eric Burkhart
Dill Harris: Walter Drake
Tom Robinson: Steve Nomoki
Heck Tate: Chris Collins

Bob Ewell: Holden McCabe

Maude Atkinson: Mary Matatta

Judge Taylor: Billy Carlson

Reverend Sykes: Alex Boerum

TOWNSPEOPLE/SUPPORTING ROLES:

Daniel Dirkson

Lisa Newcomb

Isabelle Mercer-Crow

Courtney Reynolds

Tom Copeland

Eva Stark

Beth Quinlin

Peter Niles

Samantha Francisco

Rachel Lordes

Deborah Wagstaff

Julia Parks

Beth Canody

Ariane Neville

Cisco,

Did you see it??? Did you see the list???? Well I won't tell you everything in case you didn't, but I'll tell you this: I GOT SCOUT!!! I GOT SCOUT!!! I GOT SCOUT!!!! I GOT SCOUT!!!!

I hope it's OK I told you that before you saw the list (or maybe you've seen it). Anyway, I've never been so happy in my whole life! I worked so hard for that part, and I had a heavy road to hoe because Mrs. P. saw me as a comedic actress only and I proved her wrong. And Chase THE STONE FOX of all STONE FOXES is the assistant director! We have to think of a different nickname for Chase because M.M. is the Stone Fox AND MAYBE YOUR BOYFRIEND!!! WE CAN'T FORGET TO MENTION THAT!! So, what should Chase be . . . ? Hmmm. I can't think right now, Señor Snyder is going to give us a pop quiz any second—I know because Ariane has Spanish before me, so she warned me. Long live the secret agents!!

Love,
Bean

Bean!!!

Yay! CLINK! CLINK! CLINK!!!

I'm toasting my invisible chalice to your success—you deserve it! And yes, I did see the list and see that I am townsperson number 3. Yay! All the girls got parts! We're all in it again! M.M. is *not* my boyfriend. Some walking and kissing does not a boyfriend make. Although when you say that, I get all swoony and full of hot air (not gas) and start to rise out of my seat like the boy at the end of *The Red Balloon,* where all the balloons cluster to him and lift him way up high!!! Oh, I'm a dork! An incredibly happy dork!

Happy days are here, my Beanster!!!!

I'll see you in the Little Theater after school for the run-through, *Scout!!!* You TOTALLY FLARP!!

Scoutalicious!

The Scoutster!!

The Scout-Bean!

Love,
Cisco

Cisco,

Long time no write! I'm bummed that you and the rest of the townspeople aren't at most of the rehearsals so far. It's not the same without you and the girls there. Except thank God Myrna's Mayella Ewell. Andrew Pease makes an excellent Jem; we're having fun rehearsing together. I actually know most of my lines because I studied the scenes so much for the auditions. Chase is very impressed. Oh my gosh—I love him! He's a great director, but he's also really silly like us. The other day Mrs. P. had him run a scene with Jem and me while she did some office work, and he's pushing us for more emotional realism, working our tails off, and suddenly in the middle of the scene, he throws a banana peel at us and it hits Andrew on the side of the head! I laughed so hard I almost peed. I wish he wasn't so much older than me or I'd ask him to marry me. I'd drive up in my mom's old paneled station wagon all decorated with crepe paper, shaving cream, and a big JUST MARRIED scrawled on the side, and I'd pull up in front of Chase, wink at him (I've been practicing Ariane's technique), and be like, "Hop on in, Sailor!!"

NOT!

But it'd make a good story someday. And I'm all for doing things just so it'd make a good story someday. Maybe we could incorporate that into Flirt Club? Besides Flirt Practice we should all do something together purely for the sake of being able to tell a story about it someday.

Write me back—I miss you even though I see you every day at lunch!

Bean

Bean,

I know! We haven't been writing enough. So guess what? You know how last night Michael and I went to Lyon's after school? Well he asked me to go steady! We were talking about Mia and Scott and how they made a good couple, and he goes, "So, are *we* a couple?" And I totally blush and shrug my shoulders. I didn't know what to say—doesn't the guy usually ask the girl to go steady? We've hung out three times now and talked at our lockers, but I haven't really known what he's thinking. So then he goes, "So, what does a guy have to do to get to be your boyfriend?" And I just look up at him (totally red in the face, I'm sure!) and go, "Just ask," and kind of shrug.

He smiles and twists a piece of my hair around his fingers (swoon!) and says, "Izzy Mercer-Crow, will you be mine?" and I'm so overcome I just nod. And he kisses me! In a public place! He's not embarrassed to be seen with me! Doesn't he know that I'm a drama geek? And yes, let's have Flirt Club this weekend, Mrs. Chase Matthews, *and* yes, let's definitely do something just because it would make a great story someday—I love that idea.

Love,
Cisco

Cisco,

Oh my eyes are so starry and dewy from reading your note! It was so romantic! He actually said, "Will you be mine?" Oh my Gump . . . sighh . . . And right in time for Valentine's Day! I feel all puffed up with romantic mist! I'm being serious even though I sound silly. You are a Cinderella mermaid—it's so romantic, my fingers are damp and tingly! I know someday something that romantic will happen to me too. It's sort of like *Gone with the Wind* but totally different. You are Melanie who DESERVES Ashley Wilkes because you're so beautiful and good that you shine like a dewdrop!

OK, I'll shut up now, I'm gushing. And Shelly would be Scarlett though Michael doesn't secretly yearn for Shelly the way Ashley does for Scarlett because you are a mermaid princess. Who shines like a dewdrop! Sighhhh. I have rehearsals EVERY DAY this week. I miss you! But I love rehearsals. Being Scout is sort of hard because I'm supposed to be a kid but I don't want to come across as false or fakey-cute. Mrs. P. is helping me tremendously. She says to be as real as possible but to think about being innocent and wide open. Not cute and diminutive. She's smart. And Chase is one handsome motherflupper!

Well, I'll get to see you this weekend for Flirt Club. At Myrna's right?

Love,
Mrs. Chase Matthews
Please incinerate or eat or flush this note IMMEDIATELY!

~~~~~~

Izzy's Journal

I think I'm happier than I've ever been before in my whole life. I might be falling in love with Michael. I don't really know since I've never been that way before. In love that is. Happier but also more miserable. And I can't share my misery with my friends OR ANYONE! Because they are the cause of it. Well, THEY aren't but here's the problem: After Michael asked me to go steady with him, he asked me why I didn't eat lunch with him. (I didn't tell Annie about this part of the conversation—I never could.) I shrugged and said that he and I were in different groups. And he said, "Groups schmoops," and would I please eat lunch with him. I said, "Well, I can't very well just abandon my friends!" And he said, "So your friends are more important to you than I am?" And I said, "NO! Of course not. But I would feel really bad if I didn't eat lunch with them." And I said, "I don't really know the people you eat lunch with." And he said, "Well how are you going to get to know my friends if you don't spend time with them?" I said, "I'd love to spend time with your friends but maybe just not at lunch." And then he got kind of quiet and he didn't hold my hand as much and stuff AND I FELT SO GUILTY! He did kiss me good-bye when he walked me home. (Sigh!) And as he left, he goes, "OK, see you tomorrow *at lunch.*"

I really don't know what to do. I feel so confused. I can't leave Annie and the girls at lunch—that's the only time I see them except for Flirt Club these days. 'Cause we're not rehearsing the scenes with the townspeople yet. I don't know what to do. I wish I could talk to someone, but the usual person I'd talk to would be Annie. And I know it'd kill her if I sat with the popular people. Here I have an invitation, practically a *command,* to sit with the popular people and I'm miserable. And, you know, come to think of it . . . why can't he come sit with US at lunch if he wants to eat with me? Is it that he really wants a girlfriend who's part of the popular group? Is that important to him? I wish I had the nerve to talk to him about this. Tomorrow's Friday. So, I only have one more day before the weekend to be tortured about what to do at lunch hour. Maybe I'll go to the library and pretend I have to study for U.S. History. We do have a test. Of course I know the material like the back of my hand, but it never hurts to review stuff. This sucks.

13

"The Worst Day of My Short and Uneventful Life"

Cisco,

I thought you had to study during lunch. Why were you with Michael at the popular table when I was going to my locker? You don't have to lie to me if you want to eat with him. He is your boyfriend now, after all.

Bean

Bean,

I didn't lie to you! I know it seems like I did, but I didn't! I wouldn't ever, I promise! I WAS in the library and Michael knew that, and when lunch was almost over he came in and *dragged* me out to go sit with him for a little! I'd never lie to you, Bean! Please believe me.

Cisco

Cisco,

Don't worry about it. I know you probably want to eat with your boyfriend/the popular people now. You don't have to make excuses (go to the library or whatever). You should be able to eat wherever you want.

Bean

Bean,

I WANT to eat with my best friend, YOU, and maybe *sometimes* eat with Michael. BUT I didn't say I had to go to the library so I could eat with him instead. It *wasn't* an excuse. You believe me, right?

Cisco

~~~~~~

Izzy's Journal

Oh God, today was the worst day of my short and uneventful life. I went to the library at lunch as planned and told both Annie and Michael that's where I'd be. And then at 12:25, Michael comes sneaking up behind my table and grabs me from behind and starts whispering in my ear, etc., to come outside with him AND he's got his arms wrapped around me from behind and starts to drag me out of my chair. Literally. So

I give in and go outside to eat with him (I was starving too), and he plops me down next to him at the popular table. Everyone is being pretty nice, especially Annette and Jason. And it *would* have been kind of thrilling to be eating at the popular table except that I wanted to sink into the wood under my butt and die because I was terrified that Annie or one of the girls would see me. And she did! I guess she passed by on the way to her locker though I didn't see her. And I got that awful note right before U.S. History and almost started to cry in class and had to excuse myself to the bathroom 'cause I was so upset that tears kept leaking out of my eyes every minute or so.

Annie's been my best friend forever and for her to think I'd *lied* just to sit at the popular table with Michael is unbearable. Her next note was better but not much. And then *total silence* after I sent her my last note asking her if she believed me. TOTAL SILENCE.

Even if she didn't get my note till 7th period, she would have called right after school if she wasn't mad. She must be mad. I can't stand it! And now *I'm* kind of mad. How can she not believe me? Maybe she's feeling weird that I'm going out with this popular guy? Or mad at me? I DON'T KNOW HOW SHE FEELS 'CAUSE SHE DIDN'T WRITE ME BACK! I don't know what to do. Maybe I could talk to Mom. Though I haven't really confided in her as much over the last couple of years. It *seems* like Annie doesn't believe me and I really CAN'T believe *that*. Flup. I want to go to Flirt Club tomorrow at Myrna's but I feel weird since it seems like Annie isn't talking to me????? I guess I won't go.

Flup.

~~~~~~

<u>The Seventh Official Meeting of Flirt Club</u>

Members present:

Ariane

Lisa

Myrna

Annie (me)

Izzy, absent :(

First order of business: Time for Toasts!

We toasted me getting Scout with our invisible chalices—*CLINK! CLINK! CLINK!*

New Techniques: No one had any new techniques to report this week, BUT Lisa brought the shirt she designed AND sewed for Myrna for her to try on. It was soo adorable and sexy but kind of edgy still. Perfect for Myrna. She modeled it for us on a pretend runway while we sang that song "You Sexy Thing" by Hot Chocolate.

Flirting Activity Reports:

Ariane: As usual things were very fruitful in Ariane's sector. She has a new bevy of male friends because of OPERATION

WINK AT THE WHOLE WORLD. Including Danny Rosenberg, Glenn Gould, Rick Carlson, Jeff Turner, and Greg Prentice. They all wave to her in the halls and scurry to catch up with her if they're going to the same class. Some of those boys have starting eating near us at lunch, and Glenn and Danny actually joined us without an invitation on Wednesday and Friday last week!

Unfortunately, Ariane doesn't like any of these boys more than friends, but as she said, "You never know . . . attraction can grow out of a melding of mind, heart, and spirit." Ha-ha! (She read this in one of her mom's self-help books.) Apparently Ariane's mom (who is single and trying to meet boys, well men, too) offered to come to Flirt Club and give us some pointers!! Ariane said that she *didn't* tell her Mom about Flirt Club (as per rule number one, two, and three!) *but* she told her that we met sometimes as a sort of support group for shy girls. That was nice of Ariane's mom, but we decided not to take her up on her offer because we like our group the way it is. Plus, Lisa couldn't stop laughing about it, and she says she's afraid she'd laugh out of control if Mrs. Neville, I mean, Ms. Carlson (she recently took back her maiden name), came to Flirt Club.

ANYWAY, a wee bit of concern was expressed that Ariane aka Twitchy the Winker is turning into a player. This made **her** giggle uncontrollably and then start walking around the room like a cowboy with extra-heavy spurs on.

Myrna: On a more practical note, Myrna has struck up a

conversation twice in rehearsal with Toby McGuinty. Her specific techniques: The first time she asked him about his sneakers and if the shoelaces were sold separately (nice one!). The second time she asked him to run lines with her while they weren't on stage. Brilliant! We had a round of toasting with our invisible chalices to Myrna's bold conversational skills!

CLINK! CLINK! CLINK!

I told her that I liked Toby McGuinty too, you know in a "from across the room" sort of way. So we threw down our invisible gauntlets and said may the best woman win!

(What's a gauntlet anyway?)

Lisa and I had nothing to report. Lisa says she's still as shy as a lamppost.

I had no progress to report. I have had my hands full with Scout and haven't been thinking about boys much. Because I've been thinking about a MAN! Chase Matthews to be more precise!

Ariane called him a "savory MANWICH."

We toasted to Chase Matthews the SAVORY MANWICH, CLINK! CLINK! CLINK!

Practice session: Today's practice session was a double whammy because we decided to also implement the "doing something that would make a good story" idea. So we dressed up as boys (AND MEN! ARIANE AND LISA PUT ON SOME OF MYRNA'S DAD'S OLD SUITS!) and went to the movies at the Old Mill. Now, it could have been counterproductive dressing up as boys and then going to the Old Mill to *flirt* with boys. But we managed it! How? Well, we're high-jinxing, double-daring double-agents, that's how! This totally cute boy was getting our popcorn and candy and Myrna (the cheeky devil) pushes Lisa in front of us all against the counter and goes to the totally cute counter boy, "My friend here has a question for you." And the counter boy goes, "How can I help you, sir?" and winks at Lisa! So our costumes actually HELPED our cause versus HINDERING it. Well, Lisa turned about 100 shades of red and goes, "What's that tattoo on your arm?" Smarty pants Lisa! I hadn't even noticed the guy's tattoo, it was barely peeking out of his shirt sleeve. So he flashed us his tattoo and he talked to Lisa about his "peregrine" for a hefty minute or so and how he had to cover it up at work, etc. (Luckily no one was behind us in line.)

Then he gave us snacks but didn't charge us the full amount and WINKED AT LISA AGAIN AS WE WALKED AWAY!

Love is in the air! Being a cross-dressing double agent flarps!

What we all want to know is what's a peregrine?

OK. We looked it up. It's a peregrine *falcon* (not to be confused with the *Millennium Falcon*), and it's like a hawk. Lisa was right. (I thought it was a mythical creature.) FLIRT CLUB IS SO EDUCATIONAL! Aren't we a bunch of ornithologists! We decided that Flirt Club is from here on out to be referred to as Ornithology Club. It's our new deep cover.

Then, since tomorrow is Valentine's Day and none of us

have boyfriends, we made each other valentines with glitter and collage stuff. Long live arts and crafts!

And thus concluded the 7th official meeting of the Ornithology Club!

~~~~~~

Annie-Bean's Journal

Flirt Club was fun, as usual. But my heart is heavy. I can't believe Izzy didn't even come. Well, I sort of can. I mean, I didn't respond to her last note and she probably thinks I'm mad. And I am a little, but mostly I just feel weird. That whole library thing was weird—I don't know what to think. What if she's done with being a drama geek/secret agent and is just going to be one of the popular people now? I would die if that happened.

Honestly, I was hoping she'd come today (or at least call), and we could talk about it or NOT talk about it and just try to put the whole thing behind us. Of course, the girls asked where she was, and I just said I didn't know; I didn't want to get into the gory details. One thing I won't ever do is talk about Izzy behind her back.

~~~~~~

Izzy's Journal

Sunday Night—I have a stomachache. I didn't go to Flirt Club yesterday and none of the girls called me. What if they all hate me now? I thought for sure Annie would've called by now. We've gotten in fights before but they never last. (Once in 4th grade we were mad at each other for a whole afternoon.) I'm still tortured about the where-to-eat-lunch thing. I'm not sure if I'm *welcome* to eat with Annie and them, but if I eat with Michael it may confirm Annie's idea that I lied so that I could eat with him instead of her! I really just want to call her and clear things up, BUT SHE SHOULD CALL ME!!

I feel like I'm going to explode—this is too confusing for me.

On a *much* happier note, I hung out at Michael's tonight for Valentine's and it was great. He gave me one red rose and I gave him a bag of those candy hearts that say things on them (lame, I know, but I had NO idea what to get a boy for Valentine's Day). He didn't bring up the lunch table thing at all. We watched a movie on the couch (his parents were out to dinner), and every time he came across a candy heart that said "kiss me" on it, he gave it to me! So, we kept ending up making out. My tongue still knows what to do! Woo-hoo! And he felt me up! I *hate* that phrase as much as I hate the phrase "second base." So unromantic! How would Jane Austen have referred to that sort of activity? Hmmm, she wouldn't have. I don't think they felt each other up in those days unless they were married and maybe not even then? But it was fun all right, even if Jane wouldn't approve.

His dad drove me home when they got back and he's super

nice. So is his Mom. They have a nice house. They are definitely richer than we are but not snobs. One thing bugged me though. There was a picture (among a lot of other pictures) on the refrigerator of Michael with Shelly Scott. Why does he still have a picture of her on the fridge? I've seen her in the halls a few times, but she totally ignores me as she's always done. Why do I feel like some kind of infiltrator with that popular group? Like I've done something bad by going out with one of *their* guys? Like I don't know my place or something. Mia and Madison WERE weird when I sat at their table on Friday for all of ten minutes. They were superficially friendly, but something in their voices, their eyes, was like, "Intruder alert, intruder alert." There's this underlying coldness under the surface niceness, though you can barely call it niceness. Annette Angelo, though, seemed genuinely warm at lunch and at the party. Shelly wasn't even there, thank God. This is too weird. I didn't really ask to become a social experiment: Can the drama geek cross the impenetrable boundary of the popular crowd? All I really want is to hang out comfortably with Michael AND my friends. I want to have enough time for both and NOT HAVE TO CHOOSE!

I don't know what I'm gonna do tomorrow. I can't pretend I have to study in the library again. Oh God, my stomach hurts. I wish I had someone to talk to. Annie, I wish I could talk to Annie. Maybe she'll write me a note tomorrow and everything will be OK. I will make her a collage and put it in her locker first thing.

@ @ @

Izzy's Journal

I kept racing to my locker all day today, hoping for a note from Annie. But nothing. My life is so bizarre. I survived lunchtime but barely. When the bell rang I still didn't know where I was going to eat and was considering going out to the field and eating alone. I was actually more nervous than when I was doing my monologue for my *Mockingbird* audition. I was standing in line at the snack bar when someone came and put their hands over my eyes from behind. It was Lisa, sweet Lisa! And we hugged and giggled, and she told me all about Flirt Club AND cross-dressing! (I missed SO MUCH!) So, she's obviously not mad at me. THANK YOU GOD OF SMALL FAVORS AND SNACK BAR LINES!

After we got our food, she linked elbows with me and started walking to our table so I let myself be led. (Though I was so nervous to see Annie, I felt weak-kneed.) When we got there, all the girls (and Danny and Glenn) were perfectly friendly, but not Annie. She gave me a stiff smile and a cool, quiet "hi." Luckily Myrna, Ariane, and Lisa were chatting away so constantly about the cross-dressing adventure that the silence between Annie and me wasn't really that obvious.

SO THEN, halfway through lunch, Michael comes over to our table (we were sitting on the opposite side of Center Quad so he had to come looking for me) AND PICKS ME UP! He goes, "Excuse me, ladies, but I'm going to steal Izzy for a bit," and he *carries* me slung over his shoulder across Center Quad! Everyone, I mean EVERYONE saw. I was embarrassed but also secretly thrilled! And guilty—did I mention guilty? Can't forget THAT emotion; that's a constant one in the swarming pool of emotions that I seem to be drowning in these days. I also felt the tiniest bit miffed. He didn't ask me to come sit with him and basically forced me to, and it would have been nice to have a choice. But at least this way I felt less guilty about sitting away from the girls.

SO, I ended up spending the second half of lunch at the popular table next to Michael, which was fun. I get terribly melty around him. I mostly talked to just him. Mia and Madison TOTALLY ignored me today, not even a hello! Seems like everywhere I go these days, someone is giving me the cold shoulder. The boys were nice and so was Annette, as usual. Annette's goofy! She kept sneaking up behind Michael and me and singing cheesy love songs in a totally smarmy lounge-singer voice. Annette cracks me up! She'd fit right in at Flirt Club. And Shelly was at the table with Mia and Madison. She didn't look at me even. That's probably why they ignore me. For her sake. Well, that and the fact that they seem to want nothing to do with me! Ugh. I hope Annie's not *more* mad that I spent half my lunch with Michael.

What will I do tomorrow? Besides get an ulcer from the stress of my life? I really do actually feel sick.

Maybe I'll stay home.

14

Invisible Chalk Circles

Dear Ariane,

Hey, guess what? Margaret Pope heard about our cross-dressing escapade! Apparently her little brother saw us at the Old Mill. She asked if we were going to do it again and could she join us! Ha-ha, we're famous! I'm so glad we're gonna start rehearsing the courtroom scene next week so you girls will be at rehearsals finally. Sisters of the Corn reunited!

Can you believe Glenn Gould and Danny Rosenberg? Eating with us now as if we're all old friends. Ariane, you kind of have a harem—a harem of sort of nerdy boys! I'm just hoping that since these guys eat with us sometimes, maybe we can rope Toby McGuinty on over too. Yee-haw! Got my lasso! Git my spurs! I'm gonna wrangle me some Toby McGuinty for lunch! Now THAT would be a Story Worth Telling—if I actually DID lasso Toby McGuinty and drag him to our table. I bet you or Myrna would do something like that—you're getting so bold it's almost scary!

Goan now, git me ma spurs,
Annie

Dear Annie,

I goin ta git you dem spurs and goan git cha sumpin elsin dat ya bean needin all right . . . and dats sum dis here chew, plat I meen splat, whoopin sorry, I spit on yer shoo.

Sorry der, cowgurl,
Ariane

P.S. Izzy must be sick, she wasn't in French.

Dear Ari,

I cain't unnerstan a word uv ya!

Annie

Dear Annie,

An I cain't git chur wurds n'stuffin meself.

Ariane

Izzy's Journal

Well, that's two days down this week, three more to go. This is ridiculous though, I can't pretend I'm sick (although my stomach really feels awful) for the rest of the year because I don't know what to do at lunchtime. I really need to talk to someone. I can't talk to Michael about it 'cause he'd just be like, "Well, eat with me! There, it's settled!"

Michael called after school to say hi, etc. Oh, I'm a dreamy, dew-eyed blob when I think of him! Annie did not call. It really seems like she doesn't want to be friends anymore. I am simultaneously the most miserable and the happiest I've ever been in my life. I am considering talking to the school counselor, that's how bad it is. I wonder what an ulcer feels like and if I have one.

~~Izzy,~~

Where WERE you at lunch? I looked all over for you but then gave up.

Meet me at my locker after 7th. I'll walk you home.

~Michael

M,

I'll be there.

~*Iz*

~~~~~~

Izzy (Cisco)'s Journal

I can't really believe it but I actually went to see the school counselor, Mr. Dorfman, at lunch. Partially because I couldn't deal with trying to choose between eating with the girls or at the popular table, and partially because I feel like I'm having a nervous breakdown. My stomach feels like it's full of butter-flies constantly and half the time those butterflies are on fire. I can hardly eat. Mr. Dorfman is really sweet. He sat there eating a brown bag lunch "that my wife, Clarissa, was kind enough to pack for me." He ate an egg-salad sandwich that kind of kept dangling from his extra bushy mustache. He's sort of nerdy but has such kind brown eyes. He just chewed and nodded while I babbled on about Annie and Michael. I felt strangely comfort-able. He kept dabbing the corners of his mouth daintily with a cloth napkin Clarissa had packed for him, completely ignorant of the fact that most of the egg salad was in his mustache!

After one thorough dabbing session, he told me that it sounded like Annie and I were very dear friends who loved each other very much and that some communication might be in order. I started to cry when he said that, and he handed me his cloth napkin with egg salad on it (ick!) 'cause there were no Kleenexes! When he saw the egg-smeared edge of the napkin he turned it around so I could use the clean side!

He just sat quietly nodding while I cried (he momentarily stopped eating) and then he said, "I applaud your willingness to express your feelings, young lady," and he was so dorkily earnest and nice that I started to laugh-cry instead of cry. And he giggled too and he had egg salad in his teeth (gross!) but I still really like Mr. Dorfman. Egg teeth and all.

When Michael and I walked home I didn't tell him about it. I said I was in the office at lunch because I didn't feel well (that part is true!). My stomach hurts way less tonight and I think it's because of talking to Mr. Dorfman. I think he's right, that Annie and I need to talk. But I wrote her that last note AND made her a collage. She should come to me. Or write. Maybe she just doesn't want to be friends anymore. We're rehearsing the courtroom scene next week, so we'll be in each other's faces. That could be weird. I've decided that I'm going to eat with Michael tomorrow and Friday. *He's* the one acting like he cares about me.

@ @ @

Izzy's Journal Monday

My mom just knocked on the door and told me Annie's on the phone (my cell is OFF), but I told her I couldn't talk. Not after what happened in rehearsal today. Plus, my nose is all stuffy from crying, and I DON'T want her to know she made me cry. I really didn't think she could do something that mean. Can't write right now, too upset.

@ @ @

Mom just knocked AGAIN, says Annie's on the phone and really wants to talk. I just can't. I made her go away. But I think I can write about it now, my eyes have stopped leaking for a bit. Oh God. We were at rehearsal for the courtroom scene and all of us Sisters of the Corn were offstage for a bit so we were all sitting together chatting (except Annie and I weren't really talking directly to each other), and Willy Collins came up and started talking about auditions for the next community theater production (he heard it was *Camelot* for sure, NOT *Godspell*). THEN he started talking about when Annie and I sang the duet "By My Side" from Godspell for the 6th-grade talent show and how good we were. SO the girls and Willy started pushing us to do it for them! What a nightmare. I'm pretty sure this is what Mrs. Kelly was trying to teach us is *ironic*. I literally lost my power of speech momentarily and just turned red.

They wouldn't let up, so finally Annie goes, "OK, *OK!*" sort of angry-like, and we started singing and it seemed to be going all right, but then halfway through Annie just stops cold and quickly walks away, without a word.

I think it was the worst moment of my life.

Everyone just stood there looking totally shocked. I turned totally red and before I could stop them, tears started pouring out my eyes. The girls tried to hug me and stuff, but I couldn't deal. I just grabbed my backpack and said to tell Mrs. P. I was sick and I just left. I came home and I was sort of numb for a while, and then I started crying and haven't been able to stop. I'm so sad. We've been singing that duet together for years—it's like OUR song—and she just walked away. I am so humiliated. My mom keeps wanting to come in too, but I want to be alone.

Dear Cisco,

Please read this! I know you didn't want to talk on the phone last night and I can understand why. But please hear me out. I KNOW you probably think I walked away from our duet yesterday because I was mad at you.

But that's not true!

I walked away because I felt myself starting to cry, and I knew if I continued, I would have burst into tears. I am so sorry I just walked away. Myrna told me YOU started to cry. I feel so bad.

Oh Cisco.

I have never been so miserable in my life. I'm sorry for walking away, and I'm sorry for being a butthead in general. I know I haven't written you or called or anything. I know in my heart that you didn't lie about going to the library—you ARE Melanie from *Gone With the Wind* AND Eliza Bennett from *Pride and Prejudice* and don't have any lies in you. I think I *thought* I was mad, but I was actually *scared*. Scared that now you're with Michael, you won't want to be friends anymore or be in our group. That you'd leave us to be in the popular group. I guess I kind of was dissing you first so you wouldn't do it to me. I know. I'm such a dumb-head. Me and my stupid red-haired temper! Anyway, I hope you will forgive me. I love you and I MISS YOU!!!

Love forever (even if you hate me now),
Bean

P.S. I hope you know that if we were ever to not be friends it would break my bootstraps once and for all.

Dearest Bean,

I forgive you. I'm sorry I couldn't talk on the phone last night, I was too upset. Thank you for explaining everything, I FEEL SO MUCH BETTER!!! I'm so glad you don't hate me!

I was so relieved to get your note I had to go sit in a bathroom stall because my eyes were leaking and I had to collect myself before I could go to French.

I know the library thing was weird. I WAS in there studying when Michael dragged me out. But *part* of why I was there is that I was so confused about where to eat. I want to eat with you both AND I don't want to hurt anyone's feelings. I'm such a boob, and **I** AM SORRY I didn't just talk to you about it. I just hid in the library like a little weenie in a bun! I would never not want to be friends. And even if I hang out with Michael at school sometimes, I WILL ALWAYS spend time with you and the girls too.

You guys are my rock of Gibraltar, my bread and butter, my pride and joy, my relish and mustard! Did you know I was so upset about this whole thing that I went to see MR. DORFMAN??? You (and Mr. Dorfman) are the only ones who know this TOP SECRET INFO. He's actually *really* nice! Remind me to tell you a story about egg salad and an overly large mustache. My life is so much more fun when I can tell you all the gory details! Like M.M. grabbed my b***s! Well, it was more pleasant than "grabbing"! He's the artful grabber!

Love, love, love,
Cisco

Cisco,

Let us never let this happen again, this strange estrangement, OK, my little weenie?

I KNOW! My life doesn't really feel likes it's happened until I can tell you about it! I can't wait to hear about egg salad, mustaches, and artful grabbing! (I have something to tell you about boobs too, but it is TOP SECRET!)

As far as lunch, it sounds great if you eat with us sometimes and Michael sometimes.

I'd better go.

Love,
Bean

P.S. Write back if you can today and let me know what the popular lunch table is like. Is there a fresh scent in the air? Are you blinded by all the blond hair reflecting the sun so brilliantly due to super expensive hair products? Do the popular people move in slow motion like they always do in teenage movies? Do they use the freshest, most up-and-coming slang? Like *flarp*? (NOT!) Do they ever spill food on themselves? Never, I'm sure. They live in vacuum-packed bubbles!

(FEED THIS NOTE TO A PAPER-EATING PLANT!!!)

Dearest Bean,

That sounds good about lunch. I love hanging out with Michael, BUT I have more fun with you guys than the popular people. There's not much to tell about their table except that Michael's thigh is a gift from heaven when it's warmly snuggled next to mine!

Ahhh! I'm a huge mushpot, like in ring-around-the-rosies! Annette Angelo is really nice and funny. So are some of the boys. The other girls basically ignore me and that is slightly painful. I feel a little like a pariah or an intruder when I'm with those people. But a pariah in heaven because of Michael! I can't wait for rehearsals today. I am definitely trying out for *Camelot*. I'm so glad you encouraged me to do drama this year, Bean.

Love,
Cisco

P.S. You're the best girl ever.

~~~~~~

Izzy (Cisco)'s Journal

Oh thank Gump and thank the stars, thanks to the bumpy orange bedspread under my tummy, thanks to the bookshelf full of tattered old books that Annie and I cleared things up. My stomach has finally stopped hurting. AND I've stopped fearing the lunch hour like the plague. I wish Michael would actually eat with us sometimes. Somehow I doubt that . . . I don't think he wants to give up his status as popular boy! He'd rather raise MY status to popular girl. I don't know how I feel about that. I'm never gonna abandon the drama group entirely, ever. Why does it have to be like this? All these stupid groups . . . having to be in one or the other. Why can't people just have friends? Why are things so rigid? It's like there's these chalk outlines that follow us wherever we go and people in other groups aren't supposed to cross those lines. I mean, if I think about it, I, myself, have never crossed that line into the popular group. Only when Michael has carried me or led me across. Or when Myrna threw a French fry across.

It seems like the more cool the group, the more important the line is. Like thanks to Ariane's winking, Danny and Glenn eat with us now, and they just plop their butts right on down next to us with no compunction. That's good—I hope people feel like there's NO chalk circle around our group.

15

Underwear Wedgie, Underwear Wedgie

Cisco,

I didn't tell you before, but when we were fighting (or not talking), Elvis got really stubborn and hardly ever left the building. And, well, you know how that can make me toot a little more than average. Well, once at rehearsals when we were rehearsing the scene where I bend over and pull something out of the knothole in the tree, I let one rip. Totally by accident. Chase laughed so hard he fell off his chair. And Toby yelled from off stage, "Gazuntight!"!!! Not as bad as when snot flew out of your face, but still pretty bad.

Bean

Cisco,

Isn't Toby cute? Doesn't he make a good Atticus Finch? I mean, he even kind of looks like Gregory Peck with those cute glasses. Sigh.

Bean

Cisco,

I am so glad that we're all at rehearsals together this week. The Sisters of the Corn kick buttocks! Guess who ate with us today . . . Toby McGuinty! Ariane hollered at him as he was passing by. She goes, "Hey!" (He keeps walking.) "Hey you, Mr. Toby!" (He stops and looks at us.) "Hey, Tobster!" She YELLS, "Come on down!" Like he was on a game show or something. (Can you believe her? We've created a monster!) So he walks over and he goes, "Yes?" kind of shy-like, and Ariane goes, "Have a seat young man, make yourself at home!" and he just laughs and DOES IT!

Anyway, it was really fun 'cause he's so cute and silly, although Glenn and Danny looked a little miffed. (I think they're OK with their polygamous platonic relationship with Ariane if they are number one and number two but not if there're any other contenders!) Actually, Toby mostly talked to me about the show and stuff and GUESS WHAT? He's trying out for *Camelot* too! Apparently he sings. We all started interrupting each other with our favorite songs from musicals, and he sang "Oh God . . . I'm Dying" from *Godspell* when Jesus is dying—you know that one? It's so beautiful and sad and he sounded like heaven. I can't believe it! As Ariane said, where've you been hiding that voice, Toby McGuinty? And he said, "Oh, in the shower." He's funny. And cute. And my new husband.

Next week is tech and dress and all that, so I'll see you almost every day. Yee-haw!

Also, also, also, it's Flower Day NEXT FRIDAY. I don't think we need to do what we did last flower day—you know, our secret undercover flower-sending mission? We don't need to do that this time, do we?

Love,
Bean

Bean aka Agent #66,

It sounds like you guys had so much fun at lunch. I miss you guys! I've been glued to Michael's side lately, I know, I'm sorry, but I think I might be falling in l***!! Shhh, don't tell a soul—that's a super undercover secret. The popular table is not all it's cracked up to be, I'll say that. Just because they all look like they walked out of a magazine doesn't make lunch any more interesting or my food taste better. Yes, I agree about

Flower Day—I think we'll be OK this time around, I don't see any imminent humiliation on the horizon. Yay! I get to see you at rehearsals, Mrs. McGuinty!

Love,
Cisco aka #88

P.S. Maybe we can write our flower cards up at Flirt Club on Saturday?

P.P.S. Is Ariane becoming a player? Should we be worried?

P.P.P.S. You are SO good as Scout, I can't believe I know you because I know one day you'll be famous.

@ @ @

Flirt Club Minutes—The EIGHTH Official Meeting of Flirt Club!

Present: All (Myrna, Lisa, Ariane, Izzy, and Annie, me, the scribe)

Only one thing to report: Apparently a couple of people have started calling Ariane "Winky." Margaret Pope did, *Chase Matthews* did (!), AND some people Ariane doesn't even know said, "Hi, Winky," when they passed her in the hallway. Her Ninja Winking is getting some attention, apparently. Ariane is not sure if this is a good or bad thing.

We unanimously decided to forgo our usual Flirt Club

structure to write our flower note cards for Flower Day (they're going to be *green* carnations this time around, I guess 'cause it's getting close to St. Paddy's Day? Or spring is almost here? As Myrna profoundly mentioned, I hope they don't look like lettuce). I am writing one to Toby McGuinty (so's Myrna—we threw down the invisible gauntlet again!), but I think I'm actually going to sign mine this time. Not signing Enrique's card was probably a mistake that doomed my relationship with his ear. We decided to actually sign all the cards we send as ourselves this time.

CARPET DIEM!!!!

~~~~~~

Flower Notes

Dear Toby aka Atticus,
It has been so fun being in the play with you!
~Annie
P.S. You have fantastic hair.

(Possibly a little boring but nice, plus a tiny bit of silliness/ flirting.)

Dear Toby,
You are as handsome as Gregory Peck.
Love,
Myrna

(Too flirty for comfort!)

Dear Toby aka Atticus,
Your stern but compassionate manner in the court-
room scene sends my southern heart aflutter like a
white hanky being waved by the Confederate army
when they knew they were beat.
Sincerely,
~Myrna aka Mayella Ewell

It's clever and flirty without being too much so—I wish I'd thought of it myself! Ah well, that's the gauntlet for you. Myrna and I shook hands and pinky swore that if either of us were to actually date Toby McGuinty, the other one would instantly forgive the other, pick the invisible gauntlet up, and dust it off.

Dear Michael,
I am so glad I've gotten to know you!
Love,
Your Stalk of Corn, Izzy

It actually took Izzy about an hour to write that! Oh brother. She didn't want to be too mushy or lovey-dovey nor did she want to be all stiff and formal. Then she debated for half an hour whether to include the "Love" part or if she should write "your loving stalk of corn" because she didn't want to freak out Michael by mentioning love. We asked if she did love him and she said YES. That comes as no surprise to me since she's adored him since kindergarten as far as I can tell!

Ariane did some damage control since her winking seems to have caused some confusion among the men-folk at Wilbur Middle School:

Dear Glenn,
I am glad that we're friends.
Your friend,
Ariane

Dear Danny,
I am glad to be friends.
Your friend,
Ariane

Then we decided we had to send at least ONE covert, un-signed card because we are secret agents, after all, so we're sending one as a group to Toby that just says:

I Loved You Once in Silence

That's it.

We decided on Toby because:

A. We all agree he's a Stone Fox (in a Clark-Kent-who's-actually-Superman kind of way).

B. He'll get the reference (it's Guenevere's song to Lancelot in *Camelot*).

Oh, I love mischief! Oh, how I love it!

Lisa is just sending flowers to girls 'cause there ain't no boys she wants to send any to. The above flower-card notes are the only ones worth mentioning in Flirt Club minutes. Of course, we're sending flowers to each other, but we didn't show those notes.

I wish I could send one to Chase Matthew. I wish he went to our school. SIGH.

And thus concludes our eighth official meeting of Flirt Club.

Long live Flirt Club!

Annie-Bean's Diary

Oh my Gump, I love Flirt Club. Because of all the rehearsals and having Flirt Club, this week was just like old times. Things have been pretty different with Izzy going out with Michael. We don't see each other as much or write as many notes etc . . . I guess that's what happens when your best friend starts going out with one of the most popular guys in the school!

Lately, she usually eats lunch with him at the popular table . . . she hangs out with us, too, but she eats with us less and less. Mostly I feel fine about it all, or that's what I tell myself, but I think it's harder on me than I let on. Even to myself sometimes. I'm kind of jealous (even though I'm also totally happy for her), AND the worst thing is I miss her. Sometimes I put a note in her locker and don't get one back for a while or ever sometimes. Thank God for the play. And that I am Scout! Rehearsals are my home away from home. Mrs. P. and Chase are so cool.

Izzy WAS really helpful when I was trying to compose a flower note to Toby. Sigh . . . he's cute AND talented. I think that talent is probably the most attractive thing for me in a guy. I'm so excited for opening night.

OK, I have to write about this 'cause I haven't been able to talk to anyone about it, BUT the weirdest thing has been happening: My boobs are growing! When I got the part of Scout, I was sort of small chested and my body was sort of boyish, so that's good as far as playing a kid. So then suddenly in the last couple of months, my boobs have gotten bigger and don't look too boyish anymore—it's so weird! I had to go bra shopping with my mom and get a C cup instead of my usual A! The new bra is a little big, but at the rate I'm going, it won't be for long!

Oh brother, I'd be a little excited about it if I weren't playing Scout. I keep wearing baggy T-shirts and hoodies so people (especially Mrs. P.) won't notice. Not that she'd be like, "Annie! You've grown boobs! You're fired!" But I feel a little guilty. And a little pleased, honestly! I'm getting all mermaidy like Izzy. If I were Jeannie Mateo right about now, I'd start wearing tight, low-cut shirts that are all sparkly or leopardy. But I'm not!

Although maybe after the show is over I'll get some cute shirts that are a little tighter. It's kind of fun having boobs. I sort of feel like a wrapped Christmas present and maybe I'll unwrap a little when *Mockingbird*'s over. Where'd these boobs come from, anyway? My mom and sis have 'em; I just thought the boob gene skipped me. Guess not!

@ @ @

Dear Bean,

You know how Michael came to our open tech rehearsal? Well, he said that you were probably the most talented actress in the school! I agree, you rock! I mean, you flarp! Annette Angelo said you were great too when we were talking about it at lunch. They didn't even mention my stellar performance as Townsperson Number Three! I mean, I think I delivered my lines—"Carrots and peas, carrots and peas!" and "Rutabaga, rutabaga, rutabaga"—brilliantly! Of course, no one can hear what we murmuring townspeople are saying, exactly, but isn't it strange that again my acting fate revolves around vegetables?

Mrs. P. says that those are the standard lines for a murmuring crowd, and that cracks me up! But you know some of those boys in that courtroom scene are NOT murmuring "Carrots and peas" or "Rutabaga, rutabaga"! Tom Copeland and Peter Niles were saying naughty things to try to get us girls to laugh. They'd better not do that in the dress rehearsal tomorrow or any of the real shows. Things like "underwear wedgie, underwear wedgie" and "pinching the wiener, pinching the wiener." I kept my concentration even though we had so many students watching! All those concentration games like Big Booty, etc., that Mrs. P. makes us play are for something after all.

I love my townslady dress—the full long skirt and calico print! I wish it was still the style for women to wear long dresses. I can't believe Flower Day AND opening night are on Friday! Just two days away! Right on! Or "Right arm," as Annette always says. I bet my socks that Toby McGuinty sends you a flower. He is always gazing at you in rehearsals!

Love,
Cisco

Dear Cisco,
Toby is "gazing" at me because we are acting in a lot of scenes together and the script demands that he gaze at me! Oh I don't want to get my hopes up about him liking me.

OK my little carrot . . .

Your devoted pea.

P.S. The Sisters of the Corn decided at lunch today that we'd all go out after the dress rehearsal tomorrow. Can you come?

Bean,

Wouldn't miss it for the world.

Love,
Cisco

~~~~~~

Izzy's Journal Friday/Opening Night

I can't believe how great this year is turning out, SO many good things for me and the Bean!

1. Flower Day was great! Michael sent me **four** flowers—each card had one letter of my name written big: I Z Z Y.

2. Annie Bean got a flower from Toby McGuinty AND he brought her a rose on opening night!

3. Opening night was great; we got a standing ovation. Of course it was mostly parents in the audience, but still!!!

4. I love Michael Maddix more and more every day! We have so much fun together.

    He's a little pushy sometimes about, well, sex stuff—so far we've only gone to 2nd base, and that's all I want to do. I mean we haven't been going out that long (even though, as he mentioned, I have known him my whole life).

Annette told me in private that he and Shelly did "everything but," which I guess means all the bases except for actually having sex! Hmmm, well, that's their business. I felt a little weird that I wrote, "Love, Izzy" on my flower card to Michael, because he didn't say anything romantic on any of my cards—just put those big letters spelling my name, which WAS romantic, I'm not complaining!!! I'm pretty sure he likes me as much as I like him . . . like, God forbid if I ever try to eat lunch with the girls, he pouts about it and says things like, "Oh well, tired of me already!" and looks all cow-eyed.

I know he's mostly joking, but I get so worried he's not and that he's really upset and that I'll lose him if I don't do what he wants! It makes my stomach all tight to think about it. I've told him he can come eat with me and the girls (and Danny and Glenn these days), and he goes, "What? You don't like my friends do you?" He twists it back on me somehow . . . so mostly I've been eating with him at the popular table because I want to spend time with him and 'cause he's so weird when I don't! I DO like his friends! Not all of them like me, *that's* for sure. Shelly has at least started smiling at me. But it's this weird hard glittering smile—there's no real friendliness—like a piece of glass got stuck on her face.

Annette and I are real friends now, I think. She may try out for *Camelot*, which would be so cool. I've noticed in general other kids at school have been treating me differently . . . as if I am one of the popular people. Girls I don't know very well tell me I look cute and smile at me in the halls and stuff. Some seventh-grade boys whistle at me, try to catch my eye, and make comments when I walk by in the hall! All the boys in the popular group wave and smile at me in the hall and call me "Izz." It's kind of fun, I have to admit. If I'm totally honest with myself, it's more than kind of fun—I really like it! I know it's all because of Michael and the fact that I sit at that table now. And really, it's all pretty weird—I'm the EXACT same girl I was a couple of months ago except for the fact that I part my hair on the side!

I really hope Annette tries out for *Camelot* too. AND Michael—he said he probably wouldn't because of soccer, but I hope so. Mostly because then he won't give me a hard time about how my rehearsals are keeping us apart. I don't know if I'll get a part though because it's a community theater production, NOT a school play, and there will be *much* better people trying out—people from Terman and all the private schools. Yikes. BUT the good news is Mr. Libratore is going to be the musical director, and he knows and likes my voice. PHEW!

Cisco,

Guess what, guess what? After Sunday's matinee, Toby asked me for my number—he said he wanted to see if he could borrow my *Camelot* CD, so I didn't think that much about it . . . BUT last night when my family and I got home from Lyon's, there was a message on the voicemail for me from Toby, and he didn't mention the CD at all. He wanted to know if I wanted to hang out after Friday's show!! He said maybe just he and I could go to Fenton's or something!!! I think he asked me out on a date. I can't believe it. I'm all shaky inside from happiness.

I didn't call him back because it was too late, but hopefully I'll see him at lunch today and tell him yes!! Oh my God, what if I'm about to get a boyfriend? Oh Cisco, oh the times they are changing!! Just like my dad's scratchy Dylan record says over and over again in a whiny voice!!

Oh Cisco, if Toby really likes me, then we will both be dating *boys,* actual boys. What? Us? The shy wallflowers? I know I'm getting ahead of myself. I don't really know how Toby feels.

Flush this note down the toilet, Agent 88, or crumple it up and put it in a body cavity—yuck, never mind that suggestion!!

Bean,

Oh, Bean, that's so great!! I knew all that gazing wasn't just because he plays your daddy on stage!!!

Who's your daddy?

Toby McGuinty!

Gotta go, talk soon,
Cisco

Cisco,

Well, it's official—I have a date with Toby Friday after the show! We "firmed it up" (funny phrase, huh?) at lunch. He said his dad or mom will drive us (but not come with us, of course!) since Fenton's is downtown.

Sincerely,
Mrs. Toby McGuinty

◎ ◎ ◎

Annie,

Myrna here—I am writing this note because I don't know what to do. Today during my free period (2nd) I saw something terrible. Or I think it's something terrible. I don't know what to do or even if I should write it down. You know over by the edge of the soccer field there's some gnarly old trees that are almost off campus and you can't see them unless you're on the bike path leaving school or near the end of the field? WELL, Margaret and I were sitting in the field during 2nd 'cause sometimes we like to do homework out there if it's not wet and anyway—sorry I'm taking so long to get to the point but this is awful—WE SAW M.M. (yes, Izzy's M.M.) NEXT TO THOSE TREES WITH SHELLY SCOTT.

At first I was just like, "Oh, they're talking, no big deal." But I was keeping an eye on them because they were standing pretty close to each other. The way Margaret and I were sitting, we could see them but they couldn't see us. Anyway, about halfway through the period, they started holding hands, and they were still talking.

And then they just stood with their foreheads together and held both hands.

They weren't talking anymore, they were just standing all close like that (NOT the way you'd stand with a friend!). They didn't kiss but what I saw was pretty bad and I don't know what to do . . . I've been keeping it inside all day—I didn't say anything at lunch because of those boys who eat with us now, but I needed to tell someone! What should we do? I think we should tell Izzy. I'd want to know if I was in her shoes.

I'm sorry this is such a sad note for you to receive. Please call me after school since there's no rehearsal and we can decide what to do.

Love,
Myrna

16
Trouble with a Capital T

~~~~~~

Annie-Bean's Journal

We had an emergency phone tree/conference today of Flirt Club (without Izzy). I called Myrna, who called Ariane, who called Lisa. Myrna and I came up with a plan of action because of the whole Michael Maddix/Shelly Scott thing (*if* it's a "thing"—that's the question) and passed it on to the other girls. We're going to do some reconnaissance. Some real-live spying. Myrna will see if she can track M.M. during 2nd period (his free period AND Myrna's). I will try to track him when he's at or near his locker because I have three classes near there. Ariane will watch him during 1st snack break (the rest of us have 2nd snack break), and Lisa (and everyone) will just keep their eyes and ears peeled in general. We decided we would sit near the popular table during our various free periods if any of the popular people are sitting there, to see if we overhear anything. I will also try to sit near Shelly during U.S. History (we don't have assigned seats AND she's always got a crowd of people trying to sit near her, BUT I'll do my best—see if I can overhear anything).

Jeez, this is awful. I don't really know what to do. I actually broke down and talked to my sister about it after dinner. On one hand I feel I should tell Izzy right away and let her decide what she wants to do . . . but as Deb pointed out, there may be nothing going on, just a little affection between two friends who used to be boyfriend and girlfriend?

I don't know, it seems pretty weird to me. I wish I had more experience with boyfriends and "relationships." That doesn't really seem normal to me, but I don't know what's normal at all, do I? I know if M.M. was MY boyfriend and he was hand-holding, forehead-smushing with Shelly, I'd feel weird about it.

Talk about weird . . . I am so happy because of Toby and the play, BUT simultaneously I'm sad because of this weird (maybe) thing with Michael and Shelly. The girls will report anything worth reporting (about our spy mission involving M.M.) through locker notes (my locker has been dubbed HEADQUARTERS) and phone calls after school. This is one of those times I wish we could use our cell phones at school. Or carry walkie-talkies. THAT would be fun. We could be all, "Breaker-breaker, 10-4 good buddy, what's your 20?" "Roger that, Mama Bear, this is Little Bo Peep in the southwest pasture, got a copy on the DT, over and out."

"Kshhhh."

We can't really talk about our mission at lunch 'cause of the boys who eat with us. At the beginning of the year it was just me and Izzy in our oddball twosome—now there's the girls and Glenn and Danny and Toby, and some of the other townspeople have been eating with us since *Mockingbird* opened. It's super fun.

How weird is that? Life is weird. Middle school is weirder!

~~~~~~

Reconnaissance Reports for the Week

Annie,

I successfully followed the subject during our free period and have nothing to report—no suspicious activities. The subject spent time with Jason B., throwing those little black berries at the abandoned portable near the Language Arts wing. They made lots of dark splotches and smudges on the side of said wall. Then they got snack bar food, ate it, and leafed through their binders. Near the end of the period, they meandered toward the gym. No news is good news!

Myrna

Annie aka Agent #88,

First snack break was fairly uneventful. M.M. DID eat an ice cream sandwich with S.S., BUT they were with a large group of 8 to 10 people and didn't sit next to each other.

Agent #59
aka Ariane aka townsperson
number 5

Annie,

I observed our subject talking to our other subject (S.S.) in between periods 3 and 4. They were talking at a normal distance from each other and never touched. Phew.

Love,
Lisa

Dear Agent #88 or whatever
number you are,

During 2nd period I observed S.S. sitting with M.M. and Jason at the popular table for about 2 minutes. Jason sat between S.S. and M.M. so they never touched or put their foreheads together or anything close to it. She then abruptly stood up and went to the ladies' room and never came back.

Sincerely,
Myrna aka Agent #22 or whatever
number I am

Agent #88,

During first snack nothing unusual was observed. M.M. did eat a snack next to S.S. but again they were in the middle of a big crowd of popular people. They didn't act flirty or anything.

Agent #59

Annie,

Nothing to report (thankfully).

Lisa

Myrna,

Well, maybe we've been barking up the wrong tree as far as the M.M. and S.S. situation. I hope so, I hope so, I hope so with all my heart. Tomorrow night is my date with Toby. I am so excited I could pee. Literally, I've been peeing all day. When I get nervous that happens sometimes. Do you know I've never been on a date before? This is the first date of my life!

Love,
Annie

Dear Annie,

I am so excited for you! Yes, thank God we haven't seen anything weird all week. Sometimes I still feel like I should tell

Izzy what I saw??? Anyway, I won't bother you with my confusion; you deserve unblemished happiness!

I can't wait for the show tomorrow night. We should have a full house—Izzy said that Michael and all his friends are coming AND there's a big group of high school kids coming because Tom the Townsperson's big brother is coming and he's a senior at Paly and he's bringing all his friends.

Love,
Myrna

~~~~~~

Izzy (Cisco)'s Journal

I'm worried that Michael may be mad at me. He's been kind of distant . . . a little less affectionate and he only wanted to hang out with me once so far this week after school and usually we see each other at least every other day outside of school, even if it's just him walking me home or having a long phone conversation before bed. I don't think he's called me once this week. I'm probably just being paranoid. It's weird, though, 'cause Annette Angelo has been really nice this week but also kind of quiet. And today she said a strange thing. She said, "You know, even if you weren't going out with Michael we could still be friends." It was so nice I felt like I might cry. But she didn't look at me when she said it, and *why did she say that?*

I'm so excited Michael and them are coming to the show

tomorrow night (they only saw the crappy tech rehearsal) and then we're all going out afterward. I'm gonna invite the girls—I don't care if it puts a wrinkle in the popular girls' underwear, that's their problem. Although Annie has other plans! I'm so glad she has her Toby date!

@ @ @

Annie,

I spoke too soon. I saw something awful again. I had to stay late after 1st-period science because I didn't understand one of the test questions at all and Mr. Peterson was trying to help me. So I left about 15 minutes late. I took the shortcut through the field because I was way over in the portables. *Anyway,* I passed by those same craggy trees near the end of the field, and M.M. and S.S. were there again, and they didn't see me because I was walking up behind their backs, and AGAIN they were holding hands and talking, but this time that wasn't all. They totally had no idea I was there and I heard Shelly say, "'Cause you know I'm not gonna wait that much longer," and he goes, "I know," and *kisses her*! At first it was not directly on the mouth but on the corner of her mouth and then she leaned in and gave him a real kiss on the mouth that he happily returned. CAN YOU BELIEVE IT!!

The flupping butthead!

I froze like a rabbit and turned around and quietly walked back the way I'd come & they never saw me. I had to take the long way around. But now we've definitely got to tell Izzy. What about tonight after the show? I don't want to freak her out right before she's supposed to perform. But she's supposed to go out with M.M. after the show and she should know before then. I want her to break up with him before he gets the chance to break up with her!

OOOH—I hope she dumps his ass!

Mad Mad Myrna

P.S. Sorry to have to report this on your happy day, I know it's gonna cloud over your sunshine!

Myrna,

Oh geez, I feel like I'm gonna burst into tears. That's awful. You did the right thing to tell me even if it makes my happy day sad.

We have to tell Izzy. We'll tell her right after the show, OK? That way, she'll be able to perform without being upset, but she won't go out with M.M. (that muther-flupper) again without knowing the truth. This is one of the weirdest days of my life. Today is one day I hope Izzy *doesn't* eat with us. It would be so hard to act like everything's OK.

With love and serious woe,
Annie

⊚ ⊚ ⊚

<u>Izzy's Journal</u>

Today was probably the worst day of my life. I woke up feeling strange. Like there was something I was supposed to remember but couldn't—just this nagging feeling inside that something wasn't right in the world but I couldn't put my finger on what it was. Lunch was really weird. Michael barely touched me and usually he's got his arm around me or holds my hand or sits really close. He didn't talk to me that much, he mostly talked to the boys, and the only person who really paid any attention to me was Annette Angelo. She was nicer to me than he was. And Shelly steered clear of the table completely, and she did yesterday, too. Michael just said very casually when the bell rang for 5th period that he'd see me at the show. He didn't talk about hanging out afterward or offer to walk me home.

Anyway, now the awful part. At the show, the girls were acting really strange, sort of extra-friendly but also kind of . . . strange. I thought maybe they were mad or it even crossed my mind that they'd had a little alcohol! But immediately after the show it all made sense 'cause Annie and Myrna pulled me out of the dressing room and into the bathroom and into one of the stalls. They proceeded to tell me that Myrna had seen Michael kiss Shelly during 2nd period and that she'd seen them together one other time too. I believed her totally. She was sure about what she saw, and she started crying when she told me 'cause she felt so bad.

I felt like my heart was going to explode in my chest. I got really hot and felt like I couldn't get enough air and I started to shake and had to sit on the toilet. I didn't feel sad right away, just totally shocked. And I still do. Feel shocked. I only started crying when I got home and into my room. I told Michael that I didn't feel well and that I needed to go home, and I didn't confront him or anything. He's probably out with Shelly and them right now. I have to break up with him. I'm not looking forward to it. I feel so stupid. Like, why did I ever think Michael Maddix would want stupid old me? I know I'm not the one who did anything wrong, but why do I feel like I did?

The girls and I made plans to hang out tomorrow and maybe Sunday, too. I'm so lucky I have such good friends. They said they'd get ice cream and popcorn and we could watch movies all day. I can't believe Michael would do that to me. But part of me expected it all along.

Dear Bean,

I still haven't confronted Michael yet. After I talked to you on the phone last night, I chickened out. I sort of can't believe he didn't call me all weekend. I thought he'd call at least to break up! Now I have to do it. At lunch if I can, because I won't be able to pretend everything is fine with him. Ever again.

Thanks for such a great weekend! That was so fun playing Poor Animal. I think it's my favorite theater game. You guys are the best and so is Jake Gyllenhaal, my new boyfriend. I may not have a real boyfriend anymore, but I have glossy hair and cool temp tattoos on my arm and belly!

Love,
Cisco

Dear Cisco,

Come sit with us after the B.U. (breakup) if you want.

Love,
Bean

Dear Bean,

It's 6th period, my free period, and I did it! I confronted him! And broke up with him. I couldn't go out to Center Quad and sit with you guys because I started crying immediately afterward and had to hide in the girls' room until 5th period.

Here's what happened: At first when I got to his lunch table, he was affectionate and pulled me to him and asked where I'd been all his life, and I literally couldn't talk. I just stood there totally silent and didn't hug him back. Shelly was at the table too but not next to Michael, the bitch! He goes, "What's up?" I shrugged (still being totally unable to talk), and my eyes got a little bit shiny from tears that wanted to come out—but I didn't let them, not at the popular table!!!

So he goes, "Come on, you, let's go talk," and we went to the field, and the walking helped because by the time we got there, I stopped being so tongue-tied. I go, "Listen Michael, I know about you and Shelly. I know you kissed her and who knows what else, and I want to break up," in this voice I didn't even know I had. It was like I had a bell in my body and it was ringing loud and clear. Weirdness! And you'll never guess what he did. He sort of fell/sat down cross-legged on the field and put his face in his hands. He didn't try to deny it or ask how I knew, he just sat there for a long time. So I sat down too. And he finally looked up—his eyes were dry, thank goodness, 'cause I thought he might be crying!—and he said, "I am so sorry, Izzy," and I was just silent. And he sort of rambled for a while about how confused he's been that he still had feelings for Shelly but didn't know what to do about it, and he didn't know if he should say anything 'cause he liked me so much and things were messed up with Shelly, and now things were messed up with me but he still really wanted to go out with me (as if!) and blah blah BLAH about his own troubles!!!!

I finally just interrupted him and said, "It sounds like you're very confused" (active listening from peer counseling in

7th grade!), and he nodded and looked like a sorrowful cow, and then he rambled some more about how difficult it is to really like two people at once (poor animal!) and blah blah blah ABOUT POOR, POOR HIM! SELFISH BOY. *Finally* he's quiet, and I just go, "Your life sounds really confusing" (more active listening!), and he nodded some more, all sad, sad puppy eyes and tried to hold my hand, but I snatched it away and go, really sarcastic, "I am so sorry that YOU are the one suffering, that YOU are the one who is SO TROUBLED, and that YOUR life is SO hard." Then I jumped up, "Well, I am going to make your life MUCH easier. I am no longer a part of it AT ALL!" And I walked away as fast as I could without running.

He called after me "Izzy!" and again "Izzy!" I kept walking (not even looking back!), and he stopped calling. Thus ends my first real relationship. Boy, I really liked him, but I feel relieved, too. He wanted me to be like him, one of his crowd. And he wanted to do more stuff (you know, sex-wise) than I was comfortable with, so now I don't have to deal with that kind of pressure anymore. Even if he had begged me to get back together I don't think I would because how could I trust him?

Anyway, blah blah blah about my torture! What about you and Toby? Are you going on any more dates?

Love,
Cisco

Dear Cisco,

I am SO, SO sorry about the whole M.M. thing. That sounds awful. I am sending you kisses of many colors, technicolor kisses, just like Joseph's coat. Let's have Flirt Club this weekend, OK? Anything you want to do to keep your mind off things, let me know, OK? Want to go to the counter at Andee's Diner after school and get milkshakes? Or go to Bergman's and hide in the clothing racks? Wiggle the clothes and make them sing to scare the shoppers? Like we did in elementary school. Maybe we could even go to Great America this weekend and yell at boys from the gondola, like we did in 6th grade. Anything you want. Just call out my name and I'll be there, and other James Taylor–esque sentiments. Including showering the people you love with love. We'll have Flirt Club this weekend, but instead of our usual flirting agenda, we'll have a "Shower Izzy with Love" agenda.

Anyway, as far as the Toby thing, it seems to be going well. He called me Sunday night and we talked for an hour. And then he asked if I wanted to do something after school this week! So I'm pretty sure that date number two is in the hole. Touchdown!

Izzy darling, I hope you're coming to the cast part Saturday after the show. I know it won't be as fun and exciting for you as the last one, with the whole closet dance and all, but it will be fun I'm sure. Chase and Mrs. P. are buying pizza for the whole cast.

Flirt Club Saturday? Should I tell the other girls?

Love,
Bean

Bean,

You are such a good friend. Flirt Club Saturday sounds perfect. And yes! Let's go to Andee's Diner for a milkshake like we used to. I now have to start using sweet, high-fat foods as a substitute for love. Right? Isn't that what we teenage girls do?

Jeez, my heart hurts. It's so hard to concentrate and we've got all these finals next week. I wrote a poem about my mutilated heart—I'll read it at Flirt Club.

Love,
Izzy

17

Hair Club for Men and Other Unwelcome Gifts

~~~~~~

<u>Ninth Official Flirt Club Meeting</u>

Minutes:

Scribe –Annie as usual!

Present –All! (Izzy's mom is giving us a ride to the theater tonight for our last show and cast party—woo-hoo!)

Today we change our usual format and forgo furthering our Flirting Skills to support Izzy after her awful breakup. Talk about a shriveled red balloon!

First order of business, Izzy read a poem that she wrote to cope with a broken heart:

"Butterfinger Boy"
You broke my heart
My very best china, shattered
Slippery, butterfinger boy
Every piece lies on the floor and grows an eye

To watch as you step blithely
Over the pieces

OucheeMama! I got chills and so did Lisa. We want her to put it in his locker, but she says she wrote it for herself, not him.

First order of business: We played with/styled Izzy's beautiful black locks and gave her a very unprofessional pedicure that involved lots of accidental tickling and painting the skin around her nails. Her pedicure looks like a toddler executed it, but that made her laugh, not cry, and that is a good thing.

Second order of business: Upon Lisa's suggestion, Izzy did a "good-bye ritual" for M.M. Lisa said that yesterday was the vernal equinox (aka first day of spring) and that it was an excellent time to purge the Old and make room for the New. So Izzy burned all the flower notes Michael had sent her (!!!!) in a metal bowl in the bathtub. She listed all the good things she would miss and cried a little :(and then all the bad things she wouldn't miss and burned both lists! Then Izzy's mom came in and got really mad about us burning stuff in the bathtub, even though it was more of a small smolder than a fire. She shooed us back to Izzy's room.

Then as we gave Izzy a manicure (we had much better luck actually getting the polish on her nails this time), Ariane stumbled upon a brilliant plan. She kept saying how Izzy should put that poem in Michael's locker and Izzy kept saying no, and then Ariane said, "You should put SOMETHING in his locker," and Lisa said (as a joke), "How about some junk mail?" And we all looked at each other and laughed, and then we hatched a devious plan—Mwa-ha-ha-ha-ha! (evil-sounding laugh)

Next week we will launch an attack upon Michael the Cheater's (NO LONGER THE STONE FOX) locker!

Here's the outline of our mission:

> On Monday: we will all keep stuffing junk mail into the slots in his locker (at bathroom breaks, between classes, etc.).
>
> Tuesday: We will put paper clips (and any other office supplies we can think of that will fit) into his locker slats—hundreds of paper clips! Mwa-ha-ha-ha-ha-ha-ha!! (more evil laughter)
>
> Wednesday: We will stuff in as many take-out menus as we possibly can, as often as we can!
>
> Thursday: Sewing and craft items! Buttons! Thread, yarn, felt scraps, etc.! (No needles or pins, though, nothing sharp!) Glitter? (We didn't come to a final decision on glitter. It can be so pesky, Izzy felt a little uncomfortable with it—SOFT-HEARTED CREATURE!

What's a little glitter in the cracks of your life compared to a broken heart?)

Friday: Friday is miscellaneous day! We will put anything and everything we can find that will fit through the locker slots. The point is to be as mysterious and annoying as possible without damaging his property.

Izzy is a little on the fence about our locker mission because she's pretty sure he'll know it's us/her. But she's mad enough that she'd like to go for it. On one condition—that we don't put in any food or anything gross or harmful. We agreed with a round of toasts with our invisible goblets.

OK, we're off to the mall—first stop, Office Depot to buy thousands of paper clips!!!!!

Mwa-ha-ha-ha-ha-ha!!!

Back from the mall. Oh we got lots of great stuff to stuff into M.M.'s locker! Including glitter—Izzy a-OK'ed glitter.

And on this devious note, we end the ninth official meeting of Flirt Club—long live Flirt Club.

Dear Beanie Baby,

The cast party was fun—you and Toby sure looked like you were having a romantic time out on Mrs. P.'s deck! Did I see some smooching? If so, you can't say you've never been kissed anymore! You HAVE to tell me if he kissed you. OK, today is junk mail day. I'm really nervous—I'm only going to do it during classes (not between!). I want to make SURE he doesn't see me. He's got 2nd period free, so that's out as he could go to his locker any minute. My palms are sweating. Thanks for being my secret-agent friend.

Love,
Cisco

Cisco,

Let mission Locker Stuff begin! I stuffed about five pieces in there during 1st period, and as I walked back to class, I saw Myrna beelining toward his locker. We started laughing uncontrollably though we were about a mile apart! I love this mission.

Agent 66

P.S. Ummmm, yes! There was a small smooch. Small but lovely. But don't tell. Yay.

Agent #66,

It's third period. I stuffed about ten pieces in already and you know what? It was hard to fit any more in! I think it's getting stuffed already! How much stuff does he keep in his locker? I wish there was some way to watch him open it. I may wander over in the vicinity of his locker when the bell rings for lunch. But I may be too chicken—he absolutely must not see me hovering!

Agent #88

Agent #88,

I have put a total of 13—count them—13 pieces of junk mail in the designated area since first period. HO-HO-HO!!! And I'm not Santa Claus! Unless I'm the Junk Mail Santa!

HO-HO-HO!
Agent Myrtle le Turtle

Cisco,

Oh my gosh. WHEN does he go to his locker? You cased the joint (the joint being his locker) before lunch and saw no activity. I followed him as planned after lunch, and he went straight to class without a stop at his locker. He must have 50 books in his backpack! Anyhoo, I also tried to stuff some more in during 5th period but could only fit 2 more pieces in after struggling for a good 3 minutes.

I think we can hold off on the stuffing for a bit since it seems to me that we've got the darn thing filled to the nth degree. I *have* to try to be around after 7th when he opens it. You should too. But we shouldn't stand together.

Bean

@ @ @

Izzy's Journal

Oh my Gump. What a day. I actually feel sort of OK for the first time since M.M. and I broke up. It was sort of terrifying and fun stuffing all that junk mail in his locker AND I guess he doesn't open his locker much all day 'cause by the end of the day it WAS STUFFED!!! And Annie, Myrna, and I managed to be close enough to see him open it (we stood far enough down the hall that he didn't notice us). This AVALANCHE of paper came pouring out when he opened it. He just stood there totally still with his feet buried in junk mail, and then he started to curse and plough through the pile that was left in his locker. He seemed mad, which scared me but also felt good I must admit. He dug it all out of his locker, got his stuff, and left. With the pile of mail just sitting on the ground. Litter bug!

I waited (and though Annie said I shouldn't, she stayed too) for about 15 minutes, until the halls had cleared out, and then we picked up the junk mail. It was scattered and had been kicked about by kids. We did it as quickly as possible and threw it away in the recycling can. I didn't want our prank to affect the janitor negatively. And Annie didn't want to leave me on my own.

Tomorrow's paper clips and office supplies!

Cisco,

Wow, paper clips are easier than junk mail. I've already emptied two boxes into the designated area and it's only second period.

Bean

Izzy,

So far I have deposited these items into the designated area—two hundred white sticky labels, two pages of labels that say "HELLO my name is," and one box of paper clips.

~ Ariane

Cisco,

I saw our Designated Target opening up his Designated Area after lunch and though it wasn't as dramatic as the junk mail avalanche, it was just as great. Paper clips fell about his feet and he looked *so confused*—it was priceless. He started picking through the various office supplies in his locker in

TOTAL BEFUDDLEMENT!! He laughed at one point—probably when he got to the "HELLO my name is" labels (that was a stroke of genius by Lisa I must say!). Ha! I wish you could've seen. We'll do more and maybe you can watch him after school.

@ @ @

Izzy (Cisco)'s Journal

Well, what a week it's been! All my teachers probably think I have a bladder infection, all the times I've asked to be excused to go to the bathroom! Watching all those office supplies rain down on him at the end of the day (from a safe distance, of course) on Tuesday was my favorite. Take-out Menu Day wasn't that eventful as we didn't have that many menus and I never got to see him open his locker that day. What cracks me up about Take-out Menu Day was that Ariane circled various items on the menus and put little comments by them like, "This is an excellent choice!" Or "Tough as an old boot, highly unrecommended!" She disguised her writing, of course. Sewing and Crafts Day was great though. It turns out stuffing yarn and dental floss and string in someone's locker isn't that easy. Glitter was troublesome—most of it ended up on the ground in front of his locker. Though Myrna was able to stuff in this WHOLE SPOOL of this stiff waxy string that she got from her dad. Miscellaneous Day was good—this is what we ended up putting in his locker that day:

> More paper clips
> A PILE of advertisements for the Hair Club
>   for Men (we swiped these from the mall)
> Some pamphlets from the Mormons
> Some tiny doll parts (Myrna's old doll—
>   though the head & body wouldn't fit, just
>   the limbs)
> Some hair nets! (Left over from my ballet
>   days!)
> Some beef jerky. Lisa broke the no-food rule
>   after consulting me because we decided
>   beef jerky isn't gooey or messy
> Some plastic ants that used to belong to Annie's
>   brother

I think that's it.

On Arts and Crafts Day, I was a little bummed to see Michael had tied various pieces of the string to himself over the course of the day. He tied some around his head, his wrist, and dangled some from a belt loop. I guess he decided to go with the flow instead of fight it. I don't know how I feel about that. I enjoyed seeing him get so mad at all that junk mail. I guess

I'm still pretty pissed at him. I mostly feel sad though. I've liked him on and off since kindergarten. I guess I idolized him and didn't think he would ever do anything like that to me. But part of me isn't surprised because he usually dates only THE MOST POPULAR GIRLS IN SCHOOL!! And that I'm not. I mean, you can take the girl out of the drama geek lunch table, but you can't take the drama geek out of the girl!

I feel sad for other reasons too. One is that I miss Annette Angelo. She was the only one of those girls at that table who actually tried to get to know me and I DIG HER! I hope she tries out for *Camelot* because I feel too shy to go talk to her now. I feel too humiliated to ever approach the popular table again. Why is that? *I* didn't cheat on *him*! I guess I never felt like anyone wanted me there but Annette and Michael anyway.

Another bummer is that for a while I got a taste of what it was like to be one of those popular people. Other people in school notice what you're doing all during lunch and snack break. People I didn't know would smile and say hello in the hall. Boys whistling, etc. It was like being a little famous or something for a very short time and now it seems to be over. People are changing already. The whole school knows I'm not with Michael anymore. Or at least I feel like they do. Most people ignore me like they used to or, even worse, they see me and quickly look away. As if I had a disease—the "Dumped by the Most Popular Guy in School" disease. Even though I dumped him! But I wouldn't have if he hadn't cheated!

Oh well, I was happy before, I'm sure I'll be happy again someday. I just miss him. God I miss him. And Annette. And all the attention. I am so glad spring break is here so for a short time I don't have to worry about seeing him in the halls with Shelly by his side. I'm gonna curl up on the couch and read all week.

These are definitely shriveled-up red balloon days.

18

He's Only the Love of My Short
and Unremarkable Life

Cisco,

Well blow me down and call me Betty! Can you believe what happened at lunch!? I almost fell over when Annette Angelo sauntered over and asked if she could sit down. She gave you a big hug and said she missed you! Not that she shouldn't—of course she'd miss you . . . I just think of her as one of those Barbie princesses, but she was so cool and funny! She knew all the lyrics to that *Auntie Mame* song! It was weird how she fit right in. WELL SHIVER ME TIMBERS, I'm still flabbergasted! Maybe she's a wanna-be drama geek!

And then at the end of lunch how she shook everyone's hand and said, "Thanks for having me" all solemn-like. She's a crack-up. Glenn and Danny were so dewy eyed and enamored! And when she did that pretend Ninja kick shriek to Danny and said, "Watch out, Rosenberg, our organization is watching you very closely." She's as crazy as we are.

Love,
Bean

Bean,

Oh, I'm glad you didn't mind her eating with us, and yeah, isn't she great? She walked me to my locker 'cause our lockers are close and she said she was so sorry about what Michael did to me and that Shelly is a bitch! She said that! I mean, aren't they friends? She said that lunch was boring and homogenous now that I was gone and would I mind if she ate with us again sometime because she'd had so much fun hanging out with us. Then she gave me her cell phone number! Can you believe it? Weird, huh, how if you're not popular you always think everything would be great and happy if you were. But there's more to it than meets the eye. Have you noticed that M.M. has been wearing a "HELLO my name is" nametag EVERY DAY this week?

Big sigh and other sounds of martyrdom,

~ Cisco

Cisco,

Can we do Flirt Club this Saturday? I know I don't really need to practice flirting since I'm DATING TOBY! (I can't believe I just said that), but I want you guys to come over. I haven't told Toby about Flirt Club. (You never told M.M., did you?) I just told him we all got together to just hang out, do girl stuff, listen to musicals . . . on a semi-regular basis. When I said that, he put his arm around me and leaned his head into mine, and said, "That's my little drama geek," and I said, "Isn't that the pot calling the kettle black?" and he said, "That's the *Titanic* calling a tugboat black." Ha-ha, my boyfriend's so funny, so cute! As I sit gazing into the puffy cloud sky over Center Quad, I bat my eyelashes and sigh a little and occasionally give a gurgling giggle even though I'm all alone. My eyes are moist with the delight of my love. My arms dangle restlessly about my writing materials as they await my lover's embrace. My mind is a bee, a fat bee that buzzes in anticipation of my lover's lovely visage! WHAT? I'm just making up flubberty flub! I do adore the Tobster, though!!

Write me back, oh mermaid of the depths!

Bean

Bean,

Love is turning you into a poet and a dewy-eyed dreamer.

Love,
Cisco

P.S. Yes to Flirt Club!

Cisco,

Yay! Flirt Club! Myrna and Lisa can come. I'll ask Ariane during 6th period. I'm glad you guys wanna meet 'cause I have something to tell everyone. A secret to reveal!

Love,
Bean

Bean!

What secret? You can't do this to me! You know how I am with secrets. Please tell me now. Can you write it in a note? You didn't have s** with Toby, did you? You'd tell me if you were gonna, right?

PLEASE TELL THIS TORTURED GIRL! Remember, I have no love life anymore, so I have to live vicariously through yours!

Cisco

Cisco!

Silly! No, I did not have s**! With Toby! All we've done is kiss. And you know how I feel about losing my virginity! It won't happen for a long time. Maybe not until I'm engaged or married. No, silly here's my secret: I've grown some boobs!!!! I'll show you guys at Flirt Club! (NOT NAKEDLY, OF

COURSE!!) Since around the time *Mockingbird* started, I've had to get all new bras—C cups instead of A cups! Granted my old bras were too small, but my boobs have suddenly grown to twice their original size! It's like I'm some mutant! Maybe there's something in our water supply, some nuclear boob-sprouting chemical!! Ha-ha!

I've been hiding them (aforementioned boobs) with layers of bagginess because during *Mockingbird* I was supposed to be playing a child on stage but mostly BECAUSE I'M EMBARRASSED!! I'm not used to boobs; I don't know what to do with them. I'm afraid to wear anything besides ginormous sweaters and my dad's old sweatshirt. Which is becoming inconvenient, seeing as how the weather's been getting warmer.

I would have told you sooner, but there was the time we weren't talking much (shall we call it "the time that must not be mentioned"?), and then there's the awkwardness of bringing up a topic like sudden boob growth. At least they're the same size now (one started out a little faster than the other, yikes!). You and Lisa will have to teach me the ways of women-with-bosoms on Saturday.

Destroy this note, please, or it will destroy me!!

Love,
Bean.

Bean,

I'm so proud of my girl!

Or should I say my *girls*?

Ha-ha! (Get it? I'm referring to your boobs as separate enti-ties, or should I say enTITies now that they're larger!) I'm sorry, no teasing—jeez, my sister teased me to kingdom come when mine grew, I should know better. But really, yay for your new boobs!!

Lordy, how dorky can I get?

No, really, we'll have to toast your bosoms with our invisible chalices on Saturday.

Destroy THIS note.

Love,
Cisco

Cisco,

I don't mind your teasing, and I shall hereby refer to my boobs as my "girls." Me and my girls are very happy that Saturday is Flirt Club—Ariane can come, so the gang's all in!!

Woo-hooop!

SINCERELY,
~A MUCH BIGGER DORK
THAN YOU ARE

Bean,

Nope.

I'm the biggest dork ever.

Cisco

P.S. But not as big as your boobs! Hahahaha!

~~~~~~

Official Flirt Club Meeting #10

Present: All!

Scribe: Annie (duh)

Rules: Number one rule of Flirt Club: Never, EVER talk about Flirt Club.

Number two rule is blah blah blah (we got it, we got it).

Minutes:

No new techniques to report. But we did talk about Operation Stuff M.M.'s Locker and laugh and laugh. Apparently M.M. has been wearing "HELLO my name is" nametags every day to school! Izzy's had no contact with our Designated Target whatsoever, so she doesn't know if he suspects that she was part of it!

Reports on Flirting Activity commenced:

Ariane: Ariane has undergone a change of heart in regard to ninja winking technique. She realized that she may have been giving some people the wrong idea and thus may be turning into a "Playa." She was tired of having stray boys start to follow her down the halls and sit next to her at lunch. We are happy to hear about Ariane's decision to surrender the ninja wink, because our lunch table is getting too crowded. Last week Kyle M., Kenji K., and Jon T. (all wink victims) ate with us on Thursday and Friday, and there was some uncomfortable jostling/jockeying to sit next to Ariane.

She is a little sad to be giving up her ninja winking/boy harem and wiped away some invisible tears and sang "Don't Cry for Me, Argentina."

Lisa: Lisa has had some tremendous progress. She has started talking to Stanley Nacek in her math class regularly. *And* they started their acquaintanceship by Lisa's using the old "throwing something harmless" technique—a wadded-up piece of paper was the bait. Now Stanley throws things at her every day! Spring is in the air! And many hurtling wadded objects! Ah, love and courtship via projectiles.

Myrna: Myrna has nothing to report except that she built a ramp for her skateboard (she is so handy) and finally got permission from her parents to try out for *Camelot*! That makes five for five!!!! They were worried about it being downtown and rehearsals finishing after dark and all, but she will always be with one if not all of us even if she is on the bus.

Izzy: Is still heartbroken and doesn't have the oomph to flirt with anyone. We tried to sing that song "Turn, Turn, Turn" to her, but it turns out we don't really know that song. Although, I did inform her that during science Enrique asked me if she had broken up with Michael Maddix. And I said yes, she had. And I told Izzy that Enrique's ear is as cute as always, even a little cuter now that his hair is long and tufty around the ear area. His hair looks like tendrils of longing . . . that's what I told her.

Annie (me): Well, I've nothing to report 'cause I HAVE A BOYFRIEND!! I CAN'T BE-LIEVE I JUST WROTE THOSE WORDS, SO I HAVE TO DO IT SOME MORE UNTIL I Believe IT! I HAVE A BOY-FRIEND, I HAVE A BOYFRIEND, I HAVE A BOYFRIEND! No, I still don't believe it, so maybe this will help

Mrs. Toby Mc Guinty
Mrs. Toby Mc Guinty
Mrs. Toby Mc Guinty
Mrs. Toby Mc Guinty
Hmmm, yes, much better!

For our practice session, we didn't feel like a field trip or actually seeing any boys, so we baked chocolate chip cookies (THEY WERE SO GOOD!) and took some down the street to Mrs. Boynton, who invited us to tea and used her pretty old-fashioned tea set. Tea tastes so good when it's in pretty, delicate cups like that! I wonder why.

And thus adjourns the tenth official meeting of Flirt Club!

~~~~~~

Izzy's Journal Sunday Night

I can't believe what just happened. I was in my room doing homework and the doorbell rings. Then my dad comes and knocks at my door, and he pokes his head into my room and very dramatically, with eyes all wild and bugging, hisses, "It's Michael—do you want to see him?" (My parents know the whole story *except* that Michael was pressuring me sexually.) And my hands start to shake and I feel so nervous I think I'll barf.

I go, "Uh, sure, Dad." And I get up and go to the door, and there he is in the flesh—Michael—just standing on the porch. I don't want him in my room/house after everything that's happened (and my parents probably don't either), so I don't invite him in. He's standing there all sheepish and looking at his feet. And he goes, "Do you want to go for a walk?" And I go, "No." Not hard or unfriendly, just a simple no. And he goes, "Well, can we sit down and talk?" So we sit on the porch and I'm silent 'cause I'm parched and shaky and what do I have to say to him anyway? Nothing.

He takes off his backpack and pulls out this big white piece of paper. And then he gives it to me, saying, "I made this for you." And it's a collage—this gigantic heart MADE OUT OF PAPER CLIPS!!! And above the heart it says, "For Izzy," and below the heart it says, "Love, M." And in the middle of the heart is one of those "HELLO my name is" stickers with "Sorry" written on it, so it says, "HELLO my name is Sorry." And I tried really hard not to, but I start to laugh sort of out of shock and nerves, PLUS: HE KNOWS! HE KNOWS IT WAS US!! I'm SO red in the face and I can't stop laughing, and he starts too, and we're both just sitting there laughing.

Finally, my dad pokes his head out and goes, "Everything OK out here?" and I can't even talk, I wave him away and nod vigorously, and Dad goes, "No one's crying?" and that makes me laugh harder. So Dad goes back in and I'm sort of hysterical now like I was outside of the closet at the *Joseph* cast party. I AM almost crying; I'm laugh-crying. There're even a few tears running down my face, which I'm trying (unsuccessfully) to hide in my knees.

Finally I get my hysteria under control (why am I such a nut job?) and I sit up and I'm just taking deep breaths and I guess my mouth must have been open a little 'cause Michael LEANS IN AND KISSES ME! Or rather leans in and sticks his tongue in my open mouth!

Bluck!

I pull away and suddenly nothing is funny at all. I say pretty harshly, "WHAT are you doing?" He starts talking about how he's sorry—he's sorry about everything. He goes on about things not working out with Shelly and how much he misses me, my silliness, my pretty face, my gorgeous hair—and here he grabs a hank of my hair and I yank it back! He doesn't get to hold a hank of my hair! ("Hank" is a weird word!) And he winds up this long-winded, meandering speech by saying that he wants me to consider dating him again!!! And that I don't have to answer him right away but would I please just think about it?

My eyes are as wide as saucers and I just shrug. And he goes, "Thank you, I really appreciate you just thinking about it"—as if I'd said I would!—"and I'm going to leave this Valentine here with you." And I say in a stony voice, "Valentine's was almost 2 months ago." And he looks me in the eye and gently touches my nose and says, very quiet, "Yes, I remember," and he's still looking in my eyes. (Oh crap.) Then he looks away and says sheepishly, "Well, then, I'll leave this very unseasonable Valentine for you." (Why does he have to be so charming?) And we stand up and he looks puppy-doggishly down at his feet, and I think, "He's still hoping I'll kiss him." (Yeah, right!)

So he looks up at me with those brown eyes and goes, "Not one little kiss?" I just shook my head, though I have to say if it was up to my *lips*, I would have definitely kissed him!

Silly, silly betraying lips! Silly Judas lips!

So he shakes my hand like I was a business associate (I felt that handshake in every cell of my body). Silly, silly cells! And he says, "Bye, Izzy Girl," and then, "Oh, and thanks for the lifetime supply of office supplies." And with that he was gone.

THEN my dad *immediately* pops out of the door like a friggin Pop-Tart out of the toaster and goes, "THAT'S MY GIRL! NO KISSES FOR CADS!" And he SMOTHERS me in a huge hug where I can't breathe! The big 'ol snoop was spying! "No kisses for cads!"

Geek!

THAT'S where I get my geekdom from!

Snoop!

So then I escape my dad's octopus arms (which, OK, I admit, I love him and his octopus arms) and came in here to write this. I'm flabbergasted, as Annie would say. I have his "Valentine" on the bed with me. I love it. It breaks my heart. I still adore him. The cad. I won't get back together with him (how could I?), but there's no harm in just considering it, for the teensiest, weensiest second. Is there? I told him I'd think about it didn't I? Actually I didn't, come to think of it . . . But I shall. He's only the love of my short and unremarkable life. I don't think I'll tell the girls about this. I know what they'd say.

Dear Cisco,

You haven't seen me yet today but prepare yourself. I am wearing a shirt of my sister's. A boob-presenting shirt. Oh, I feel like a hussy! My sister says the shirt is sexy, not slutty . . . oh jeez these weird, subtle, and endless classifications that seem to come with being a girl! I have kept my jacket on for 1st and 2nd period—I am terrified of my own bosoms it turns out. They are biological weapons! Naw, not really—*they're just my girls*! Why don't we have any classes together? I'd have the courage to unveil them if you were by my side!

My sister kept saying how boys were going to "flock to me." I'm not sure I want that now that I have Toby. I just want to be the proud, happy owner of a fairly brand-new pair of bosoms! I hope Toby doesn't get all horndog on me if I start wearing something besides baggy sweaters and hoodies, you know? He never puts any pressure on me in that realm and that's how I like it!

OMG, guess what? I saw Michael Maddix on the way to 2nd and he *smiled* at me and put his arm around me (in a buddy-buddy kind of way) and said, "How's the most talented actress in the whole school?" Unbelievable!! The nerve! Why is he kissing up to me? I just sort of slipped out of his grip like a greased piglet and mumbled something unintelligible. Then quickly turned down the nearest hallway, which led me absolutely nowhere near where I was going. I guess he doesn't want to be seen as the bad guy. Sorry, Charlie! Bad boy, bad bad boy! (said as to a naughty doggie).

Enough about boobs (mine) and boobs (Michael). I've got to study.

Love,
Bean

P.S. I am kind of dorkily excited about unveiling my boobs!
P.P.S. Blow this note up with a nuclear missile.

Bean,

The Unveiling of the Girls!
Woo-hoo!
Take your jacket off at lunch—I'll be there, plus all the Sisters of the Corn, and we'll give you moral support and

protect you from the swarming mobs of men who, according to your sister, will be hypnotized by your boobs and will thus stampede our lunch table.

Love,
Cisco

Bean,

Oh my gosh, lunch was so funny! That top your sister lent you *is* so very cute and sexy. I love that raspberry color on you. Your boobs really did grow, didn't they? But did you see Toby's face and eyes when you took off your jacket? It was like he'd seen a ghost. He just got very quiet and kept touching your hair!! He's such a gentleman. He kept trying so hard not to stare at your chest (so many boys don't even make the effort!). But his eyes kept darting down super quick even though you could tell he was trying to control them. Trying so hard to be master and commander of his roving eyeballs! And then he just sits down on the bench and stares straight ahead with his eyes glazed and his hands in his lap like it was all too much for him. He's such a sweetie! Seems like a keeper!

Glenn and Danny, on the other hand, just kept staring and addressing all their conversation to your chest! I don't even think they *know* they're staring; it's odd.

Another great thing is that you know Toby doesn't like you just for your new boobs because you didn't *have* them really when he started to like you! I think M.M. may have mostly liked me for my boobs 'cause he seemed like all he wanted to do was . . . oh, never mind.

Bleck.

Love,
Cisco

⊚ ⊚ ⊚

Cisco,

Setting my boobs free was kind of fun and scary at the same time. I don't think I'm gonna make this showing-off-the-boobs thing a regular event. Though, I do sort of enjoy the attention. Remember in the *Elephant Man* he's all, "I am not an animal! I am a human being! I am a man!" I sort of feel like that . . . "I am not a pair of boobs! I am a human being! I am a woman!"

~Bean

P.S. Guess what? Mr. Libratore told me today that if we wanted to, we could do a DUET for our *Camelot* audition because so many kids are auditioning and they have a limited amount of time. Do you want to? Your voice is better than mine but I've got stage presence! (Not that you don't—you do too.)

We could do "By My Side." Oooo, or maybe we could do "Bosom Buddies" (the key word being **"bosom"**—hahaha!). Remember that one? From *Auntie Mame*, my mom has it on vinyl?

Love again,
Bean

Bean,

I hear your cry! Please hear mine! I am also not just a pair of boobs, I am a human being! YES, I'd love to do a duet with you . . . I vote for "Bosom Buddies" from *Mame* because it's so active and character driven; the other is pretty but sort of sedate.

Love,
Cisco

@ @ @

Tuesday, Found in Izzy's Locker

HELLO my name is . . .
I miss you, Izzy

Thursday, Found in Izzy's Locker

HELLO my name is . . .
I can't stop thinking about you

Friday, Found in Izzy's Locker

HELLO my name is . . .
Izzy and I'm really hot
    And
    HELLO my name is . . .
Michael & I wonder if Izzy is
thinking about what I said

~~~~~~~~~~~~~~~~~~~~~~~~~~~~~~~~~~

Izzy's Journal

Well, flup, I don't know what to do. Michael keeps putting these nametag notes in my locker and I feel myself slipping as far as my resolve not to let him into my life again. I really still love him. His notes are so sweet and funny. But he hasn't called; he could always just call me, right? Though I guess he came over to my house and gave me a big floppy (albeit untimely) Valentine. Am I being too tough? I mean, he made a mistake kissing Shelly. But everyone makes mistakes, don't they? And it seems like he likes me as much as I like him. I can't stop thinking about him either . . . when I think about getting back together with him, I melt inside and turn into a puddle. I really, *really* wish I could kiss him. I don't feel as angry as I did before and without the anger it's hard to stay away from him. I haven't told the girls or Annie any of this; I feel weird about that. I think they'd be disappointed or mad if I got back together with him. I can understand that, since what he did was pretty bad. But I feel weird having secrets from them, like I'm not just a secret agent but a double agent. Maybe I should talk to them about it. I don't know! All of this is making my stomach hurt again. I feel pulled in different directions. Maybe I *should* give him another chance. I've liked him for sooooo long! Will I regret it if I let this opportunity slip away? Maybe I'll slip a note in his locker on Monday, asking if he wants to walk home with me. Yikes.

Tomorrow, Flirt Club at Ariane's.

19

"And Guess What? They Float!"

~~~~~~

Official Flirt Club meeting #11

Present: All

Scribe: Annie and her girls (referring here, of course, to the new members of my anatomy, my BOOBS)

Reports, techniques, etc. . . .

BLAH BLAH!!! No one feels like an official meeting today—we're off to Mayfield Mall in our matching beanies that Lisa made! Woo-hoo, I'm getting some Swedish Fish at the candy kiosk—got to feed the girls!

And thus concludes the shortest meeting of Flirt Club in the history of the world.

Annie-Bean's Journal

WOW! Everyone's gone home, it's late, and Mom and Dad want me to watch a video with them, but I've got to stay in my room and write this down. While we were at Mayfield Mall, I spied with my little eye Shelly Scott hanging out at the terrarium-like thing near the escalators *and who's she sitting with but M.M., the big Head Cheese himself.* (Cheese Head is more like it.) He's entwined his limbs around her, and he's nibbling on her ear. So I grab Izzy (who hasn't seen them yet) and yank her arm and say real loud and jolly-like, "Hey, you guys, let's go to Andee's Diner and sit at the counter!" to try to capture Izzy's attention before it's too late. BUT it *is* too late. She just stops in her tracks and is staring at M.M. and S.S. like she's seen a car wreck. Oh you should have seen her face—it was terrible. First, her eyes got really wide. And she was literally frozen; I have never seen anything like it. Then her face goes really red and then really, really white. The girls and I just watched helplessly.

Finally, I pull on her hand and say, "Come on, Iz, let's get out of here," but she pulls her hand away and goes really quiet and growly, "That bastard!" I have never, in the 10 years that I've known Izzy, heard that tone of voice from her before or heard her cuss like that! She takes her backpack off real swift and rough-like (for a minute I thought she was going to go over and throw it at them!). But she throws it to the ground and starts digging through it; she's breathing kind of heavy through her nose. Then she grabs a floppy piece of white paper—a big one with paper clips glued on it—and pulls it out of her backpack with shaky hands and then walks really fast over to M.M. and Shelly.

I am in shock and I pick up her backpack and sort of chase her. She gets to them and, quick as a weasel, Michael unwinds himself from Shelly's body and looks totally freaked out! Izzy (still with really shaky hands) tosses this floppy paperclip thing on his lap. And says very quiet but deadly, "I've thought about your proposal, Michael, and the answer is NO!" On the word "no," her voice gets really loud. I grab Izzy's hand because I can't stand seeing her alone in front of them with her hands shaking. And Shelly grabs the white thing Izzy threw at M.M. and says, "What proposal?" all hissing like a cat!

Michael is totally silent and looks like he just ate a piece of poo. Izzy says, "Oh, his proposal TO GET BACK TOGETHER." Then Shelly opens the paper and it's this huge heart made out of paper clips (!!!!), which says, "To Izzy from Michael."

"When," hisses Shelly to Michael, "did you make this?" and Izzy turns to Shelly and says, "ON TUESDAY OF LAST WEEK," *really* loud-like. A tear has slipped out of Izzy's eye, and she wipes it off super fast. Shelly stands up, RIPS the paper clip heart picture in half, and says, "You are an asshole!" to Michael. The girls and I are watching this in total shock. THEN

Izzy grabs the two halves from Shelly and *she* rips it again and throws it on the ground, and Shelly holds her hand up in the air to give Izzy a high five. Izzy is just staring at Shelly's hand in total confusion, and it finally occurs to her what Shelly wants, so she gives her a kind of awkward high five, more like a high smush.

Then Izzy just turns around without a word to Michael and walks away with all of us trotting behind her, totally confused! We walked/trotted all the way to the parking lot, and Izzy finally plopped down on the curb and started to cry. When she could talk, she told us that M.M. had been wooing her, proposing that they get back together. That paper thing was a latent Valentine/floppy love note that he'd made her out of those crazy paper clips we put in his locker!!!! And she had *assumed* (as any sane girl would) that that meant that he wasn't with Shelly anymore. But it turned out either he was looking to have TWO girlfriends at once or he was gonna dump Shelly if Izzy said yes. Boy, he really covers all his bases! What a cheese wad!

So, Izzy told us all this and said she'd been afraid to tell us because she didn't know what to do and she knew we wouldn't like the idea of her being with him. But she had been confused because she still loved him. She cried some more at that point (POOR IZ!), but then said at least now she wasn't confused anymore. Running into him all draped over Shelly like that had made things very clear for her. Then Lisa got her some

Kleenex (Lisa is always so prepared; she's like our den mother), and we all patted her back and put our arms around her and walked home. We even sang our "Hey Hey We're Alive" song, walking like the Monkees, and Izzy did the walk with us (but didn't sing). Oh, my poor, poor Izzy!! She's coming over tomorrow to practice our duet, so that'll be a good distraction.

And thus concludes the weirdest NON-meeting of Flirt Club in the whole universe!

Cisco,

Margaret told me that Walter Drake told her that he overheard Mr. Libratore himself telling Mrs. P. that our duet went great at the auditions! I thought so! Oh I hope we get called back—I hope, I hope, I hope. Are you doing OK? I passed M.M. in the hall and he had the decency to look away and look ashamed. Thank Gump he didn't try out for *Camelot*. Mr. Libratore said he'd have a copy of the callback list tomorrow after school so we don't have to go all the way downtown to the theater to see it.

Love,
Bean

Izzy's Journal

Even though it was a whole week ago that I ran into Michael with Shelly, I still feel pretty crappy. I can't believe I almost fell for his charm and trickery. I can't believe he was still with Shelly during all that—I mean, he kissed me! And all those notes!

Shelly and him aren't together anymore; I know this because she told me herself! She came up to me at lunch on Monday and said that she was glad the whole thing had happened so she knew the truth about M.M. AND she said that she was sorry that she hadn't talked to me while I'd been dating him, that she'd been jealous. (She didn't apologize for kissing him in the field when he was still dating me—but who knows? Maybe she didn't even know he was still dating me. Apparently telling the truth isn't his strong point!)

Anyway, we shook hands and she said it was a good thing I'd had that paperclip heart thing with me as proof and why did I have it anyway? And I told her I'd brought it over to Ariane's to maybe show the girls and get their advice. I told Shelly I had other incriminating notes, and she goes, "Really?" And her face looked so sad all of the sudden, instead of her usual cool, satisfied expression. I said I could show her if she wanted and she goes, "Nah . . . that's OK. I think I've seen enough." Then she goes, "If I were you, I'd just throw them away—throw them all away!" And she was right, so I did after school.

I put them in the outside garbage can.

It was so hard.

It really is totally over.

It's strange. On some level, I feel a little *better* because I'm not confused or filled with longing for M.M. anymore. His actions have successfully destroyed those feelings in me. But on some level I feel worse because he's not who I thought he was, and it makes me sad. Oh well.

There are other fish in the sea. Or as Myrna said, "There are other worms in the compost bin!" and "There are other snacks in the cupboard."

Poor Annie can't poo again because callbacks are next week. We got called back! Woo-hoo! But now we have to do a solo instead of a duet. Which is too bad because our duet rocked, if I don't say so myself! I wish we could just do it again. I am so glad Annie is my bosom buddy.

Cisco,

Enrique asked me again about you and if you'd gotten back together with Michael Maddix. He said he'd heard a rumor that you had. What? How does this stuff get started? I said no and that Michael Maddix didn't deserve you, you were way too good for the likes of him. And Enrique said, "So true, so true."

So? What about it? Do you want to go out with Enrique? All I'd have to do is tell him you're interested and the wonderland of his ear (not to mention his lovely eyes and kind heart) would be yours to explore for an eternity...please excuse my mushiness. It's just that currently I believe in LOVE!! Or at least he may be fun to hang out with at the mall or something.

Love,
Bean

Bean,

Just wait on the Enrique thing...though thanks for offering to talk to him. He doesn't sit near me anymore in English, but sometimes he walks by and darts out a hand to gently pull my hair. I like it! I get tingles on my scalp. I just still feel sad over M.M. I think I'd be a dreary date.

I can't wait for *Camelot* callbacks. How's Elvis? Is he still unwilling to leave the building? Sisters of the Corn reunited! I hope if one of us gets a part, we all get parts; it would be too weird if only some of us get cast, you know? Plus, I hope Annette Angelo gets in too! She's the bee's knees, but you, my dear, are the cat's pajamas. I, on the other hand, am the cat's tattered smoking jacket. We're still on to practice our songs for callbacks on Saturday, right? I think singing and dancing will lift my spirits.

Love,
Cisco

Cisco,

Of course we're on for Saturday. You are not the cat's tattered smoking jacket! You are the cat's sleek whiskers! You are the ant's ankles! I am the geek's elbows!

Elvis hasn't left the building for TWO DAYS! D*** Elvis! Boy, I'll be so relieved when callbacks are over, even if I don't get in the show. At least things will resume their natural flow in my bowelular area. Or what if Elvis never leaves the building? Has that ever happened to anyone? Would they do an operation?

Love,
Bean

@ @ @

Izzy's Journal

My life is such a combination of good and bad right now. The good part is that we got called back for *Camelot* (ALL OF US!) and that I think I'm starting to get over M.M. The bad part is I still miss him and feel humiliated after what he did. I still can't figure out why *I* feel ashamed when he was the one who acted poorly. I guess I imagine people at school thinking, "Of course he cheated on her, who did she think she was? She's just a drama geek." I hope no one is actually thinking that or even really knows what happened. Though

I'm sure Shelly told her friends. Anyway, in my better moments I don't think that way—I think that I'm just fine and M.M. blew it and it doesn't matter what people think. Plus, although some people ignore me now again because I'm not with Mr. Popularity, a lot of people are still really nice to me. Some of the 7th-grade boys flirt with me in the halls! And a couple of 8th-grade boys too. Jason is always super nice when I pass him in the hall. I hardly ever see M.M. in the halls these days. I think he's avoiding me. As he should! Skulking around like a dog with his tail between his legs. Actually, I really can't imagine him skulking; he's just not a skulker. "Skulk" is one of those words that if you say it a bunch of times, it starts to sound really strange.

It's weird about Shelly. We're kind of strange allies now. We don't hang out or anything, but every time she passes me she gives me a high five. We have some strange bond now from being burned by the same boy. And Annette Angelo eats at our table sometimes, and once Shelly came and sat next to Annette! She just chatted casually with us all like it wasn't the weirdest thing in the world to be eating with the drama geeks!

I'm also a wee bit excited because I have a plan. I am going to ask Enrique out. I'm not going to tell anyone in case I lose my nerve. But I do like him. He's so nice and silly; he's taken to passing me notes again. On Friday he passed a note that said, "Izzy, I miss sitting behind your hair, your hair is like the midnight sky and now you have taken away the stars." How sweet is that? I sent him a note saying, "Mrs. Kelly and her new seating chart have taken away the stars, but my hair misses you too!" So I figure I'll send him a note asking him to go to Mayfield Mall and throw Swedish Fish in the fountain to see if they'll swim, like he suggested at the beginning of the year.

Tomorrow we're all gonna practice for callbacks and sing all the *Camelot* songs a hundred times!

Dear Cisco,

Oh, flup. The most embarrassing thing that has ever happened to me in my entire life just happened. I will tell you but don't tell another soul (not even the Sisters of the Corn). Well, Elvis left the building this weekend a couple of times, but now he seems to be stuck again, so I was alone in the girls' bathroom during my free period, *forever,* trying to move things along. Without really thinking, I started singing, "Push it good, push it real good," by Salt 'n' Pepa. So I'm sitting there for about a minute just singing to myself (instrumentals included), AND SUDDENLY A TOILET FLUSHES. Cathy Greenwood had been two stalls over (I recognized Cathy's shoes at the sinks.)

I was so embarrassed I literally broke out in a sweat. Did you know your whole body can blush? Not just your face? After this trauma, it's possible my bowels will never move again.

I know we always joke about destroying our notes BUT

REALLY AND TRULY DESTROY THIS. Wednesday is callbacks and hopefully after that, Elvis will stop being such a bad boy. I hope you don't take your own poop for granted. I hope you know how lucky you are to have regular and obedient bowels!!!!

Love,
Bean

Bean,

Oh. My. Gump.
I can't believe that happened to you.
And oh, I do, I do (know how lucky I am).

In gratitude for my poop,
Cisco

(P.S. Yr last note—totally destroyed.)

Enrique,

I have been wondering about those fish . . . if those Swedish Fish you spoke of would sink or swim if we threw them in the fountain at the mall. Do you want to try it?

Izzy

Izzy,

I too have been wondering about those multicolored fish for many long months now. I am so glad you suggested this little experiment/adventure. Would sometime this weekend be a good time to throw fish in the fountain in the name of science?

Enrique

Enrique,

I am available this Saturday in the name of science.

Izzy

Bean,

GUESS WHAT?! I have a kind of date with Enrique on Saturday! We're going to the Mayfield Mall to buy candy and throw it in the fountain! My stomach is all discombobulated, like it's full of wiggling worms—gummy worms!

~Cisco

Cisco,

Woo-hoo! Yoop-dee-yayay! Lots of geeky celebratory noises!

Wow, maybe if you and Enrique start dating, you, me, Toby, and him could all hang out sometime! And here's something else to celebrate: Elvis left the building during 6th period! Everything's coming up roses. (Or, I should say, *out* roses.) Though those roses *were not particularly fragrant!* I am so glad I no longer look pregnant!

Enough about my poo. Tell me about yours! (Joking.) My palms are sweating 'cause of callbacks!

Love,
Bean

Bean,

I'm so happy Elvis left the building! And you didn't look pregnant! You'll do great today!

Love,
Cisco

@ @ @

CAST LIST FOR *CAMELOT*:
King Arthur: Nicky Anderson
Guenevere: Annie Myers
Lancelot Du Lac: Andrew Pease

Mordred: Ron Stricklin
King Pellinore: Chris Collins
Merlyn: David Poff
Squire Dap: Billy Carleson
Lady Anne: Ariane Neville
Morgan Le Fey: Jennifer Miles
Sir Lionel: Ben Mandras
Sir Dinadan: Walter Drake
Sir Sagramore: Ben Mandras
Lady Sybil: Emily Saunders
Tom of Warwick: Bryan Jordon
King Arthur as a Boy: Tony Cayse
Nimue: Annette Angelo
Guilliam: Heath Thompson

CHORUS/DANCERS:
Eric Stark
Rob Stone
Will Wright
Myrna Mendez
Isabelle Mercer-Crow
Lyssa Smith
Lisa Newcomb
Brad Thornton
Toby McGuinty

Cisco,

I literally feel like I stuck my finger in a socket—my whole body is buzzing. I can't believe I got Guenevere, AND BEST OF ALL, we all got parts. We're all together again, AND Annette Angelo is in it too. That's so great 'cause as previously mentioned, she's the bee's knees! Our first rehearsal/meeting is Friday. Let's all go together. Maybe we could all take the 88 bus? Myrna said her dad may drive us all, but I'd actually rather take the bus. We're going to go through the songs Friday, get assigned lines, etc...

I AM SO SCARED TO SING MY SOLOS!! This is a whole new ball game. There are kids from Terman and Harker Academy in this show. It will be nice to play a part where I don't have to hide my bosoms! I bet Guenevere had some bosoms!

Love,
Bean

Bean,

I bet she did have her some bosoms.

And: WOOOOOOOOOOOOOOOOOOOOOOOOOO
OOOOOOOOOOOOOOOOOOOOOOOOOOOOOO
OOOOOOOOOOOOOOOOOOOOOOOOOOOOoooo
oooooOOOOOOOOOOOOOOOOOOOOOOooooooooo
OOOOOOOOOOOOOOOOOPP eeeeeeeeeeeeeeeeeeeeeeeeee EE

EEEEEEEEEEEEEEEEEEEEEEEEEEEEEEEEEEEEEEEEEEE
EEEEEEEEEEE!

You deserve to be Guenevere!

Love,
Cisco

ADDENDUM

~~~~~~

Izzy's Journal

So far, *Camelot* is even more fun than *Joseph*. I like the music in *Joseph* better, but the choreography for this show is waaaay more interesting, and I'd say the cast in general is better. I've met a bunch of new people. The guy who plays King Arthur is so cute I kind of have a huge crush on him.

Enrique and I have hung out twice over the last two weekends and I have a really good time with him. I don't get too nervous and dorky around him, *phew*! We did actually throw some Swedish Fish in the fountain. And guess what? They sink. So do gummy sharks and worms and fruit sours and cinnamon bears. BUT! Malted milk balls float! Last weekend, we went to see a movie and it was fun. We didn't even hold hands or anything. He seems shy, which is good. I want to take things slow with him. I went too fast with Michael and didn't take the time to get to know him well enough. I know that sounds strange since I'd known him since kindergarten! I'm not making that mistake again. Plus, I guess I do kind of have a crush on Nicky (aka King Arthur), and I'm not sure I want to suddenly have a boyfriend again. Some nights I still cry over the Michael thing, but not very often.

I'm so happy I get to hang out with the girls after school four times a week for rehearsals. Life is getting fun again! Oh, and I sing TWO (count them, TWO) solo lines in the show.

But I'm onstage a decent amount, and I'm always in front during the dance numbers since I learn steps fast. It's so cool Toby's in it too; he and Annie are great together. Toby's one solo line is "Unmolested!" which never fails to make me and Annie giggle.

Wow. We've come such a long way from popping Mrs. Healy's fuchsias and conversing with cats.

I can't believe that after *Camelot* is over, the school year will be almost done. We'll be done with middle school forever and on to Paly High. Good Gump.

Mr. Gordon is a good director, but he's much stricter than Mrs. P. Like, we can't sit in the theater and talk while other scenes are being rehearsed. He presses his fingers to his temples and goes, "giiiIIIRRRLSSS!" when we talk, and then it gets dead silent and he goes, very quietly now, "I need *utmost* quiet to do my work. Can you understand THAT?" He really likes to vary the volume of his voice. A lot. He's super quiet then suddenly VERY LOUD!! One gets the idea that he takes his directing very seriously. The other day he said, when some people were giggling in the wings, "How, HOW can I make you understand? You are young, you are ... RAW like unmolded CLAY and I, I am a sculptor! I need UTMOST QUIET." (long dramatic silent pause) "**UTMOST** QUIET, if we are to create something beautiful!!" And he sounded sort of teary on "beautiful"! Like he might cry! Talk about drama!

Of course, now every time we girls pass each other in the hall, we press our fingers to our temples and squinch our brows and say, "UTMOST QUIET!" Anyway, I have to stop writing 'cause Elvis is trying to leave the building.

GOFISH

QUESTIONS FOR THE AUTHOR

Cathleen Daly

© Anne Fitzmaurice

What did you want to be when you grew up?
I wanted to be a ballerina for awhile, then a writer, then an actress, and then a writer again!

When did you realize you wanted to be a writer?
In fourth grade. A friend and I used to go to the library with blank journals and write novels. Mine were mostly about melancholy ballerinas with long dark tresses and names like Dorian or Callista.

What's your favorite childhood memory?
One of my favorite childhood memories is going with a friend to the Christmas tree lot and hiding in the crates that held the trees and shaking the trees while simultaneously singing in an operatic voice. So it looked like the fir trees were singing opera.

What was your favorite thing about school?
The cozy corner aka reading nook. It was full of enormous pillows; big puffy pillows were big in the '70s.

What were your hobbies as a kid? What are your hobbies now?

As a kid I wrote stories or skits and then directed the neighborhood kids in them. We did a very broad interpretation of *The Parent Trap* that involved washing someone's hair with a raw egg on stage. Another hobby I had as a very young kid was building little rooms for fairies in our yard with sticks, flower petals, doll furniture, and whatever else I could get my hands on. I'd make the rooms very plush and comfortable, and locate them near windows to try to catch a glimpse of the fairies lounging. My hobbies now really vary; I love reading and writing poetry.

What was your first job, and what was your "worst" job?

My first job was in a silk warehouse, manhandling huge bolts of fabric. I don't have a lot of upper-body strength and I didn't last very long there. The worst job I had was an all-night gig blowing up balloons in a huge warehouse. The balloons were to decorate the city for the reintroduction of the cable cars in San Francisco. The helium made a high-pitched whine as hundreds of balloons were being filled throughout the warehouse. On top of that, balloons were popping and exploding left and right. It was nightmarish. But also kind of surreal and funny.

Where do you write your books?

I write my books where I live, in a peaceful garden cottage in Berkeley.

What sparked your imagination for *Flirt Club*?

Well, it's based on a lot of the actual experiences and friendships I had as an eigth-grader. Also, I love writing in the epistolary (letter) format.

Of the books you've written, which is your favorite?
My picture book, *Prudence Wants a Pet*.

What's your idea of fun?
Playing the card game golf. Karaoke. Eating a big meringue.
Reading a good book. Being in water.

What's your favorite song?
My favorite song is "The Whole Wide Sky" by a singer-songwriter
named Jhene Canody. I am lucky enough to know her!

Who is your favorite fictional character?
I have a lot of favorites. Some that come to mind are Inigo Mon-
toya in *The Princess Bride*, Chance the Gardener in *Being There*,
Officer Shrift in *The Phantom Tollbooth*, and the little prince of
The Little Prince.

What was your favorite book when you were a kid?
If I had to choose one, I'd have to say *Go, Dog. Go!* I *still* think
about that big party on top of a tree at the end of the book with
all those multicolored dogs having a good time. I want to go to
that party.

What's your favorite TV show or movie?
Again, I have a lot of favorites. . . . If I had to pick a favorite current TV show it'd be *Curb Your Enthusiasm*, and my favorite
movie would be *The Science of Sleep*.

**If you were stranded on a desert island, who would
you want for company?**
Larry David.

If you could travel anywhere in the world, where would you go and what would you do?
I would go to a tropical paradise; really, any tropical paradise would do. I'd lounge around on the sand and in hammocks and such. Eat some papayas.

What's the best advice you have ever received about writing?
Anne Lamott's advice about giving yourself permission to write really bad first drafts. She suggests writing completely freely at first and just getting it out on the page—even if it's not very good—and then reworking it. That has been really freeing for me.

Do you ever get writer's block? What do you do to get back on track?
Yes, definitely. To get back on track I still sit down at my desk regularly with whatever manuscript I'm working on. Even if nothing worthwhile comes out. Even if I just stare at my computer. Eventually something shifts.

What would you do if you ever stopped writing?
I'd probably get too many cats and become a Cat Lady.

What do you like best about yourself?
Probably that I know how to relate to cats and children, because cats and children are the creatures I admire the most on the planet.